EVERYTHING
UNSEEN

Everything Unseen by KJ Jackson ©2024

First Edition.

Sky Diamond Press
Editor: Les Plesko
Editor: Robyn Conley

What If? Publishing:
Managing Editor: Robin Shukle
Design: Liz Mrofka

Printed by: Kindle Direct Publishing

ISBN: 979-8-218-41750-5

EVERYTHING
UNSEEN

KJ JACKSON

DEDICATION

For my Mom and Dad

CHAPTER
ONE

I wish Sam had just disappeared at sea.

I close my eyes as my chauffeured car speeds along Pacific Coast Highway and wish he'd just disappeared on one of his Saturday morning kayaks, or surfing during a storm off Big Dume—where I used to sit on the beach and watch him straddling his board, bobbing, waiting for the perfect swell. And despite the search efforts, his body would never be found. Then, I'd discover him months later, sleeping between the stilts under our house, or lost, walking along the highway up in Ventura County. When I'd call out his name, he'd look at me in confusion. Later, when I brought him home, he would touch my face or as I undressed him, my hand would run along the jagged scar on his back, and he'd realize it was me. He'd have no memory of what our life had been, but he'd know we were in love, had been since we were children.

The passing breeze blows through the car window, I pull my sweatshirt hood over my head and know I could almost function that way—with the belief that if I drove far enough along PCH, I would find him. Long hair, a wiry beard, an ash-colored blanket covering his hunched figure as he limped to the left. Half the time, I don't believe he's dead. I've never seen proof, never saw a disease take him or a bus strike him. Somebody only told me. A stranger, an accented voice on the phone. And then later, many people told me, time after time, moving mouths and voices that sounded like a deaf man whispering.

No matter how fast Scott drives, even though I'm sitting in the back, the windows blacked out, I know exactly where I am along the entire coast of Malibu. The twists of the highway are familiar and I don't need to look or guess how long until I'm home. It's exactly eighteen miles from where the 10 freeway ends at Pacific Coast Highway to my house. I stare out at the ocean, trying not to notice that I still smell like the hospital room I'd just spent two nights in—a mixture of sterile plastic and iodine.

The highway is faintly lit from homes that sit on the hills just above this stretch of town. The land curves and winds along the water, mountains shadowed against a murky navy sky. I roll down the other window even though it's early October. I open my mouth to the bitter breeze; the air is heavy and thick with salt. It's familiar; I grew up with the taste. Until this moment I hadn't realized how much the smell and flavor always centered me, even just temporarily. Being away from it so long, each mile that I traveled inland, my bearings lessoned. My internal balance faltered and then went silent.

When the car slows, we're at the Topanga Canyon stop light. The waves are softer, more diluted—an offshore break. Richard must not be too far behind us and I'm glad he had his own car at the hospital. I love to ride into Malibu alone. With each mile that passes, the fog and sea air thicken, and a calmness returns to me. For a second, I forget everything. I still see the town as if it were the first time—a little girl, lopsided pigtails, identical scabs on both knees, inched forward in the back seat, the lap belt straining my stomach, my face between my parents' shoulders.

It's nearly dark by the time we get to the center of town. The shops are closed, and the highway is quiet and empty. Some say the place seems underdeveloped compared to the rest of the county. No super store conglomerates, some small businesses still run by locals mixed with high-end stores that migrated in from the city. The quaintness draws and sustains those who live here, like being tucked away in a seaside corner, protected from the rush of urban life.

A small remodeled movie theatre's marquee lights are still on, and I spot the theatre tucked back into the edge of the parking lot. The cinema, holds a mixed blend of memories. A few of my early films were screened there. Every time I sat and watched them, I couldn't help from sliding down in my chair as the opening credits drifted onto the screen, watching and then not watching, focused on other people's profiles and their reactions, how their mouths moved into a smile or contorted into sadness. Chewing on the edge of my straw long after my diet soda was gone, I never made the connection, that the woman up there was me. She was always more beautiful than I felt, kinder or harsher or more devastating, she could do something with her eyes that I could never do.

I lean farther back in my seat and wait for my driver to make the left turn that means home. I fumble with the zipper on my sweatshirt and it catches as usual. My favorite black sweat suit with a faded pink fleur-di-li symbol on the back. The one that I've lived in for the last six months while holed up in my hotel bungalow off of Sunset Blvd. I was glad when Richard handed it to me last night as I swung my legs over the side of the hospital bed. The thought of getting back into my movie premiere dress terrified me. Its silky, beaded material felt so good when I'd first put it on over my shoulders. The way it slid onto my skin, the deep V stopping at the small of my back, and then curving over my hips, helping me for a minute, feel the part I was supposed to play. A tall, actress, dressed for a night of celebration and good fortune. How then, as the night went on, it began to feel tighter, rougher, the beading cutting into my skin, sweat beneath it, and the straps digging into my breasts until I thought I would stop breathing. If I'd had to leave the hospital in it, walk the halls, with the bottom dragging along the hard teal carpet, white hospital slipper-socks poking out from underneath—it would have been like slipping into the loss of control, the loss of Sam and reality all over again.

The car pulls off the highway, and descends into a private, gated cove. I tie my Converse laces that have slipped loose and wonder if Isabelle is already here. The sound of waves crashing distracts me and lets me know we're close. I press a button to lower the partition. "I'll get out just before my gate," I say.

"Is there a problem, Ms. Douglas?" Scott asks.

"Please call me Eva," I say.

He doesn't answer. How long has he known me? Eighteen years? Since that Halloween night Isabelle met Richard. I was fifteen, but waiting up for her. Richard and his driver, Scott, delivered her, drunk to our doorstep. I'd stared at them suspiciously, my arm outstretched across the door frame, blocking the entrance. My mother barely kept her eyes open as she slurred Richard's name and introductions, her dark hair tucked into a platinum, pixie wig and her long legs in candy cane tights. I'd thought I would never see them again, that it was just another night of flirtation with a much younger man. Another man who had fallen for her large eyes and the way she puckered her mauve mouth when she was interested in something or someone. Even at that age I knew how she worked. She walked men to the door, but she rarely let them enter. By watching, I learned about relationships and about trying to love my mother. You got to the door, it was easy, she led you there. Then it would close on the trail of her voice, an alluring and lyrical goodnight. You'd knock with pleading eyes, endless pounding to get in, until eventually the skin started to break down, tear at the knuckles.

Scott slows the car and I press the unlock button.

"I'd feel more comfortable if I took you to the door," Scott says tapping the steering wheel. "Mr. Simon will be here any minute. He stopped at CVS."

For my prescriptions. I'm annoyed he doesn't call him Richard. I hate hearing him called Mr. Simon. The formality of our names reminds me of a saleswoman who has recognized me or a reporter with a microphone crammed in my face.

"I'll walk the rest of the way." I open the door before he can answer. My legs wobble so I lean against the side of the car.

"It's been a long day, let me drive you," Scott says.

A long day? It sounds so simple stated like that. He hasn't seen the news yet or Twitter, or read the countless blogs.

"Please, Ms. Douglas," Scott says, starting to open his door. He's afraid of not following Richard's instructions, to deliver me safe and sound to the front door.

I stare at the concrete, trying to steady my breathing. "I'll tell Richard you dropped me at the front door and walked me in," I say, stepping away. He nods, gives up, closes the door and then backs up the car. I don't want him to see my face up close. Most likely my mascara has dried smeary thick lines under my eyes and my pupils might be still giant and expanded from whatever was in the I.V. drip.

I focus on the gate ahead of me. It looks like massive, protective arms wrapping the house. Had I ever taken the time to take in the house from this view? Walking up to it instead of driving, the way it situates into the cove, its back resting on the bluff, the front facing the sea, the landscape forming a cocoon around the exterior. The large porch stands twenty feet above the water with silver waves rolling and retracting beneath it. A dream house. Was once a dream house.

I have almost forgotten what it looks like. How long has it been since I was here? Six months? I'm suddenly not sure of the exact time or date. Was it April then, was it lighter in the afternoon, was it red tide? Has it been that long since I closed up this new house, the white sofa in the center of an empty front room still smelling of drying paint and sawed wood? Has it been that long since I realized Sam was never coming back to live with me here?

I squint down the hill trying to see the sand through the darkness, wanting to feel it freezing underneath my toes. The same sensation I felt when I'd first looked up at it when it was almost finished. When Sam and I stood on the beach looking at something that was finally ours together. I stood in front of him, my head leaning on his chest, his fingers weaving in and out of mine.

"Who'd have thought we'd ever get here, E," he had said that day. A tarp snapped over the roof in the wind.

"I did," I'd said. Isn't this what I'd fought for? Him, this house, a life together. Years of flying from wherever I was working to visit him on weekends. Seeing an array of relationship therapists in what seemed like the same fancy office with red drapes, and cream Persian rugs. The countless books on commitment, fear of commitment, lack of commitment, sitting home at nights when he was off "finding himself," fighting about things I swore I'd never fight about: other women that smiled at him, blonde hairs on his blue jacket hanging in the hallway closet.

"Let's stay tonight," he had said.

"We don't have a bed yet. No furniture," I said. He looked at me, shaking his head, his dark hair sweeping across his forehead, falling to the middle of his ears. His green eyes become that darker shade right before he got angry or disappointed.

"Sam," I'd said and he let go of my hand. "I want it to be just right."

"And when's that going to be?" he said and started walking away, the cuffs of his Levi's dragging on the sand, his hands buried deep in his pockets. He wasn't looking at the house anymore. As he moved farther and farther away I felt it, as if whatever tethered chord or connection that was left between us was straining, painfully snapping in quiet bursts. I couldn't do anything to stop it no matter how hard I tried. I couldn't go after him, my feet paralyzed, defeated in the freezing sand. I watched him run up the sandbar and then I looked back at our house, big and white, a solid structure. Something we built together, an attempt to strengthen us. The project that was supposed to bring us together. A new start after years of sleeping in a bungalow atop the Hollywood Hills, a king mattress on the dark bamboo floors, me trying to fit into his life, his lifestyle, what he could afford.

Richard pulls up next to me as I walk towards the house, the headlights from his car reflecting, creating fluttering circles off the steel gate.

"What are you doing out here?" he asks. He's trying not to seem pushy or concerned. He looks behind us, a reflex to check if we were followed. If press or paparazzi found my location.

"Taking my time," I say, looking straight ahead.

"Hop in," he says, an attempt to sound casual. His sunglasses sit atop of his head, forgotten there.

I open the door, the car smells new. "Is Isabelle here yet?" I ask. Did she arrive at Kennedy Airport wearing a faux fur, carrying it over her arm as she rode the escalator, refusing to step aside as people tried to pass. Did she already miss New York, her green and white tiled William Sonoma kitchen in her metropolitan CO-OP.

"Your mother's flight got in this afternoon," he says, looking in the rear-view mirror. Was he wondering like me how long we had until press got here.

I open my mouth to ask him why she didn't come straight to the hospital, but I stop, afraid my voice will shake or break mid-sentence.

He accelerates and I don't take my eyes off him. His hair is starting to gray at the temples and some is sprinkled throughout his facial hair. His white button-down shirt is rolled at both sleeves. It's the same shirt he was wearing two nights ago when he came to the hospital straight from his office. Russ had called him because he was my emergency contact. I'm guessing that when he got the call, he left in the middle of the scene he was re-writing, leaving his laptop open, the cursor still in mid-sentence, trying his best to remain composed, searching for keys that were in his pocket.

He adjusts the blazer across his lap. The top of his head almost touches the roof of the car and the veins in his forearms flex as he grips the shifter. I can't see his eyes but I know they're turquoise at night. He looks so sturdy, the only way I've ever seen him, except once. When my mother left and moved to New York, I'd showed up on his doorstep, trying not to cry, pretending that I had only lost a steady dinner companion. He had a pained expression as he invited me in. It took me awhile to figure out that the sadness on his face was because he knew what her leaving would do to me.

We pull through the gate and coast down the steep driveway. The front door is lit up and I can see lights throughout the house. "Isabelle's definitely here," I say.

"Lily's been here, too," he says. "She came this morning to get the house ready and brought some of your things. She'll be back in a few days when things settle."

When did he call her? I thought he'd been in my hospital room the whole time. He must have stepped out when I slept, after I told him I needed to come back here, to Malibu—to face things. "I'm glad Lily's coming," I say. I almost remind him she's known me thirty years. That I was five when Isabelle hired her after my father left; I was twenty-five when I realized she had had a huge hand in raising me. She was there for all the hard stuff: when I couldn't fall asleep, because Isabelle wasn't home yet; reading me *Good Night Moon* four and five times until her voice became soft and tired; showing up to 'Family Day' at my elementary school three years in a row because Isabelle had something else to do—her tag reading, "Eva's Special Person" in small print under her name. Countless mornings she took extra time to match my hair bow to the color of my knee socks, so I looked put together and doted on at home. On afternoons she picked me up from school and took me to free kids' exhibits all over Los Angeles and trips to LACMA, the Getty, the La Brea Tar Pits because I was obsessed with the drowning baby dinosaur. When she treated me to matinee movies, she always said I was more charismatic, talented and beautiful than anyone on the screen. I would nod and smile even though I didn't know what her words meant. She held my hand when we walked, always a few steps ahead, making me feel like I was her only child, even though she had four grown children spread across the country. Over the hours and years we spent together, I learned from her consistency and loyalty. That maternal love was not instinctual. It wasn't born in blood ties. It developed and existed and lived and breathed in many other forms.

Richard puts an arm around me as we walk, pulling me from my thoughts. We climb up the Spanish-style steps, their cobalt tiles and glazed Satilla are muted and dull in the darkness. I try not to focus on them or fixate; they were Sam's choice. He said it reminded him of his mother and the house she grew up in Cordova, Spain.

The rough sculptured door is bigger than I remember. I lean into Richard and can't tell whose body is more tense, his or mine. I open

14

the door, and he stays behind me, his hand on the small of my back. The white foyer is lit and the wood floors have a deep maroon gleam rising off of them. The smell of baked bread and maple syrup lingers in the hallway. Large scooped out sofas sit around a mahogany coffee table in the living room and the lavender roses create shadows against the eggshell walls.

The French doors to the patio are open, revealing a silhouetted figure, a trail of cigarette smoke above her head. I glance up at Richard, see a twitch in his jaw and his hand drops off my back. I can't see his eyes but I don't want to. It was too hard looking into them last night, in the hospital. They were red, blood shot and glazed as he squeezed my hand every time I woke up, so neither of us had to find words or try and figure out what to say.

He takes a step closer to me. "How're you holding up, kid?"

I can't tell if he's asking himself or me.

CHAPTER

TWO

I remember the first time I realized Isabelle was a woman and not just my mother or hands that lifted me into a car or a mouth that scolded me. On the day of her last high-fashion photo shoot, before she retired from modeling, I visited her on set, in a windowless warehouse on the brink of downtown Los Angeles. I knocked on her dressing room door and I heard my breath catch. She turned to see who it was, her neck barely stretched, revealing her confidence. Her skin was dewy from foundation and her eyelids glittered with gold specks. She smiled, calm, her face tilted, the oval curve of her red mouth lifted as she adjusted her shoulders. Her back slid into a v-line, a strapless sheath covering the small of it. I remember reconciling that the beautiful woman was my mother.

I look at her now, in my house, tucked in the arm of the couch, her feet curled beneath her. She looks like she hasn't aged much and still appears fifteen years younger than she is. She still tells me, she gets the occasional call to return to modeling. Her years of catalogue and print work paid our bills, kept us in small houses in expensive zip codes. Her years working for Boston Proper, J. Jill and Talbots bought her a Mercedes coupe with custom tailored sheepskin seat covers, vacations to Turks and Caicos and Restoration Hardware furniture. She watches me as Richard talks. I watch her watching me.

She looks willowy and narrow in the oversized sofa. She's five-nine—two inches shorter than me. At times, she seems a foot smaller.

Her outfit reminds me of a cold beach: faded jeans, a light blue tank top, an oatmeal hued oversized knit sweater and bare feet. She has an outfit for every occasion. What she had on usually told me what mood she was in or how close I could get. As a child I knew that an immaculately tailored black suit and straight glossy hair meant I couldn't get near her, climb on her lap or cuddle. A Herve Leger bandage dress meant she was feeling older than she was and didn't want a reminder she was thirty-one-year-old with a middle-schooler. Tonight, it's her beach house look and her "welcoming back her broken" distressed daughter look. Her dark hair is loosely gathered on top of her head, with a few strands falling along her jawline. I look for signs of her age. Her skin is wrinkling slightly around her eyes and she has deepened parenthesis lines near her full mouth. I have her lips, her features, only lighter. My father's Irish skin toned down the darkness of my mother's.

Richard is sitting stiffly in a love seat opposite her. I'm afraid to join in the conversation, wanting to prolong the inevitable turn it will take—to me. He keeps adjusting his watch, moving it up and down his wrist while he talks about his latest project. He's developing a pilot for NBC about four fallen Wall Street executives trying to rebuild their lives. He's concentrating hard, trying to remember the actors' names who are attached. As he looks up at the ceiling, he bites his lower lip and I feel bad. He never forgets things.

I let my gaze wander around the room and think how much it looks like one of my film sets or soundstages: perfectly manicured, well-lit, with everything strategically placed and positioned to simulate a house. And like the sets, no matter how much time you spent there, how much music was played, or people laughed around a dinner table, it remained cold, untouched and sterile. And just above, there was no ceiling, no roof—a dark void with gleaming silver beams, never allowing it to be a home.

Isabelle sits up straight and then leans forward. "Would you like some coffee?" she says.

"No, I'm fine, Isabelle," I say automatically.

She flinches and it takes me a while to realize it's because I said her name. Did she expect something different? I have to hold myself back, not remind her again, that I'd called her that since I was three. That she'd corrected me every time I'd said otherwise. She thought mom or mother or mama, would date her, make her older, cause her breasts to sag prematurely or make her stretch marks darker, never realizing the truth. People stared at her, envied her—a beautiful young mother, twenty-ish, coltish legs with a towheaded toddler wrapped around them.

"Tell me what the doctor said, Eva," she says, her eyes fixated on her coffee cup. She licks her lips and drums her fingers.

I look at Richard, hoping he doesn't say anything about the hospital, that he keeps our experience to ourselves. I could think of it as a time just between the two of us in a private, white sterile room. I drifted in and out of sleep under multiple thin, pale-pink blankets, his hand running through my product filled hair, then down my face, his thumb wiping away my tears, his pacing footsteps in the room, loud and echoing as I dreamed.

He meets my gaze. I wait for him to speak for me. I'm too tired to re-hash anything, still somewhere between numbness and denial.

"They kept her two nights, as you know. Ran tests," Richard says. "Everything looks fine, blood work and neurologically." He rubs his forehead.

Isabelle nods.

For a second, I feel like I'm a child again, sandwiched between two adults, my head moving back and forth waiting for the story to unfold, believing they'll tell me a happy ending if I wait long enough.

"It was just some off-the-cuff ER diagnosis," Richard says crossing his legs. "They think dehydration, physical and emotional exhaustion and, maybe a cocktail of prescriptions." He voice trails.

"And?" Isabelle asks her voice impatient. "What else."

"The psychiatrist that came mentioned some possible PTSD."

I look away because I think maybe I should be ashamed, or because I am. The visuals from my movie premiere start to come back: the fluorescent panel lights, blinding and burning my eyes, the constant humming of voices and the air so cold, my skin hurting. My own voice, shaky and hoarse, calling for Sam.

Richard's eyes are on Isabelle. She doesn't have a reaction. We both wait for one.

"But it's been a year," Isabelle says. She crosses her legs and makes circles with her foot.

"Is that the cut off point for grieving," I ask quietly, still looking out the window.

If I had been delivering that line in a movie, I would have fallen short. My tone should have been biting, attacking, my eyes should have widened. I should have stared her down, my gaze not wavering, daring a response. Instead, it came out without any fight, my eyes not meeting hers, no expression left.

"Were you on anything?" she asks, ignoring my question. Her tone is accusatory. She uncrosses her legs and leans forward in her chair, rests her elbows on her knees.

I don't answer, just stare back at her because I know it'll get to her. I look at her passively and stubbornly with a distance, a silence, something I learned by watching my father. The way I learned to fight her was by watching my father. Nobody ever infuriated her more than he did.

"Eva," she says my name as a question. "Answer me." She's suddenly impatient, not being able to stand the silence, when she usually prefers it.

Minutes go by and when I see that she's about to get up, I shake my head and say, "No, I didn't take too much of anything." It's not true. I'd had two Ativan and some tequila from the bottle Sam got from one of his friends on his thirtieth birthday. He was saving it for a special occasion that never came. There's a lot more I won't admit. How my heart was racing and then suddenly slowed so much that I couldn't feel it and I wondered if I'd run out of air. That at one point as the chauffeured car sped along the freeway en route to Westwood, I'd hiked up my dress in the car and put my head between my legs to try and control my breathing. My hands were so sweaty, the door handle kept slipping as I tried to get out when I made the driver stop for me use a bathroom. My legs trembled as I got out, unsteady, knees knocking, my muscles aching, tensing and I couldn't focus. I'd caught a glimpse of myself in the gas station bathroom. My face looked so flat, my mascara and blush were gone, cheekbones sunk, lips blood red. I couldn't make out the words of the driver as he ushered me back to the car. The terror rising as he set me back in the back seat.

Isabelle closes her sweater. "Where do we go from here?" she asks, looking down. "What was the advice?"

Is she addressing Richard or me? I put my hand on the cushion next to me, and feel the space where Sam would be. The silk brocade is wet. The doors have been open too long, sea air settling on it like a thin damp blanket.

Richard lights another cigarette. "Her doctor suggested more intensive therapy and some time away from work. Maybe a change of scenery."

I nod at whatever he says, my mind drifting back to that night. I remember getting dressed for the premiere. Looking at the gown on the hanger and hearing my stylists words, that it might look too much like the one Gigi Hadid wore two weeks earlier to the UNICEF Children's Gala. Then, there were smells of damp tropical flowers even though it was fall. I'd stared in the mirror, noticing how tan my skin had gotten even though I couldn't remember being outside in the sun. It was deep olive skin. My mother's skin. I'd played with the ends of my hair, wondering when it had grown to the middle of my back and become toffee colored. My arms looked so long and skinny and dangled lifelessly off my shoulders—like paper doll arms, attached by gold rivets. My breasts rose and fell gently. Van Morrison drifted from a speaker. I could see Sam sitting behind me, watching me, his eyes lowered, lips pressed together, waiting for me to finish painting taupe shimmer on my eyelids. His mouth slipping into a sly grin, his dark suit, his muscular legs crossed, strong legs like my father's.

Isabelle pulls a cigarette out of a silver case. "I thought you *were* in therapy, Eva." She'd quit smoking years ago. It feels like everybody's weakening.

"I was," I say, her question's shame lingering.

"I was under the impression it was helping," she says, packing the cigarette against her hand.

The tension releases from my arms, the tingling that has been there for days begins to lift, like circulation suddenly returning to a dead foot. I grab at the soft material under me and squeeze until I can feel something, until my knuckles ache.

"It was. It is helping." I think of Dr. Rose, my therapist, how in my mind, she's perfect. Nothing Isabelle can say can take away from that. Rose has wonderfully coiffed, shoulder length ash blonde hair that's always in place. Her formal attire sets the tone for structure and professionalism. She wears a different skirt suit every time I go, a loose blouse, her matching jacket hangs on the back of her desk chair. Except on Fridays, when she wears loose three-quarter length skirts and leather sandals with gold buckles and straps around the heel. She has beautiful rays of crow's feet at the corners of her eyes when she smiles and her skin is slightly tanner on her forearms from the hours she plays tennis on Wednesdays. She has a few sun spots on her hands revealing her age. I notice them every time she rests her cheek on her palm when I cry. She was grandmotherly love, or what I imagined it to be.

"You have to tell the therapist everything for it to be effective," Isabelle says. "I mean, why go?"

She's right. For a while, in the beginning, I'd tell Dr. Rose what I wanted to believe my life was. Like a movie I wished to be in, starring Sam and me. A young widow left by the love of her life with a parting gift of a baby to always remember him. Except the baby didn't make it.

Richard stands up and closes the sliding door. His black pants are wrinkled. I can see the outline of his undershirt beneath his work shirt, how it covers and accents the shape of his arms. "Isabelle, she's tired."

A large wave snaps against the shore and we all turn as if interrupted. Isabelle and I make eye contact and I know she's remembering—the sound triggering the years we lived at the beach with my father. How the waves shook our little cottage from a Baja storm. Does being at the beach remind her of the only person who ever walked away from her, breaking her record of leaving first? Like me, can she still hear his voice, soft despite his tall frame, calling us 'his girls'? Does she remember how both of us cuddled up to him on the couch when he'd bring home videos from the fluorescent lit, three-shelf movie rental place on Point Dume? We'd fight to see who could get closer, nuzzling in under his arms, his large fading tribal sun tattoo pressing against my cheek, his tee-shirt smelling of coffee beans and sand. Does she still hear him loading the Nikon, or see bags of film every time the refrigerator door opened, stuffed between milk and vitamins and leftover Greek takeout? Could she still see the collection of beer bottle caps and seashells from around the world in jars by the sink? Does she realize now that we were all kids playing house until he couldn't do it anymore?

Isabelle inhales deeply on her cigarette; her eyes close, her lower lips trembles.

Richard exhales loudly. He hadn't slept much, folded into one of the hospital recliners, his head resting on his arm or at the foot of my bed.

"We need a plan," Richard says, sitting on the arm of the sofa. "We need a plan," he says again. "Don't you agree, E?" he smiles slightly, nodding and I recognize my friend. For the past few hours his role had become blurry, confusing. His voice sterner, his shoulders tense, no hint of the man I'd come to know so well in the last couple years.

I don't want to think about last night or about having to walk outdoors. I haven't faced daylight yet. "I will handle it," I say.

"You obviously can't," Isabelle says. "Last time I was here, you were getting out of bed. You seemed okay. Moving forward. What happened?" She reaches for the lighter on the coffee table. Richard's quicker than she is and picks it up, lights it for her and then lights one for himself.

I start to answer and then stop. I'm not ready to admit anything or tell them how bad it had gotten for me. One day turned into two days in bed, then into weeks. Nights brought no sleeping or sleeping in two-hour increments, waking because I felt something on my skin. Like a wool blanket that was too heavy or sheets too sticky and hardened from sweat. Eventually, I'd unplugged all the clocks because in my mind that meant time couldn't move forward. Then, they were days I actually got out of the house. I drove the speed limit to Pavilions or CVS for wine or Epson Salts. I'd sit in the parking lot for thirty minutes having to divide myself in two—who I was and who I'd become. I'd wait for the rational side to appear that could talk me into doing normal, everyday things. And once I eventually got out of the car, I pulled my sweater or jacket so tightly across my chest because I thought if I didn't, I would be completely exposed—everyone able to see through me. But the days inside the house far outnumbered the ones outside.

"I didn't know you still smoked," I say to Richard, trying to change the subject, trying to connect to him.

He sits back in the chair. "I don't," he says, winking.

The smoke lifts and spins around Isabelle's face, the distinct smell of sugary tobacco is starting to make me sick. I look for another window to open.

"How do you feel right now?" Isabelle asks me.

"I just want to go to bed," I say.

Richard runs a hand through his hair. It's shiny and looks like it hasn't been washed in a while, the usual waves have fallen flat. "I want you to know your mother and I support you no matter what."

"What?" I say before I can stop it, I almost yelled it.

Isabelle tilts her head, as if she's confused, too.

He looks taken aback, hurt. He sits up straighter as if my voice, the surprise caused his body to react.

We look at each other. He doesn't know what to say.

Why is he suddenly speaking as if it's the two of them? As if they still have a connection or ever did? Was being in this room causing a regression of time? As far as I know, he hasn't spoken to Isabelle in years, except the occasional polite exchanges when they saw one another in passing or at an event for me. Has my current state brought them back together? I turn away, look out the window, turning away from that thought.

"I'd feel better if I stayed here with you," Isabelle says. "I can go to a hotel after that, if you want." She looks back and forth at Richard and me as if she's stumbled on to something and she's trying to figure it out.

Richard nods. "She should stay."

"I'm so glad you agree," I say, nodding, my tone harsh. He holds my gaze for a few seconds and then looks away. He's so different tonight. My mother's presence seemingly erasing anything we'd built up until now—a friendship I'd come to count on, an easiness. He keeps his distance from me on the other side of the room, overly careful not to touch me, to pass closely. His feelings, reactions, thoughts, somewhere I can't reach.

CHAPTER
THREE

"Grace is coming in the morning," I say, looking for a clock, not sure how much time has passed. Richard, Isabelle and me, still in this living room. Smoke and wine and sea air suffocate the natural smell of the house.

"She called me in the hospital, this morning," I say, and I imagine Grace frantically throwing things into a suitcase right about now. Scribbling notes of things not to forget, her short hair pulled into a ponytail that keeps falling loose. She might have been near tears, her grief resurfacing with mine.

"Are you sure that's wise?" Isabelle asks. She has taken off her sweater, her long lean arms rest on the pillows surrounding her.

I look towards the kitchen where Richard went to take a phone call. He still hasn't come back. "She's my sister-in-law, for Christ's sake. I've known her since I was ten."

Isabelle's voice quivers. "She'll remind you of Sam." She flicks her ashes in the stained glass ashtray. "Can't her visit wait a while?"

"She's already bought the ticket," I say and finally spot a small clock on a side table. "She leaves Seattle first thing in the morning." Two hours have passed since I came home and I don't know how much more I can take.

"She looks so much like Sam," Isabelle says.

"You're right," I say remembering when I first noticed that. I'd stopped in front of their house, gotten off my bike and watched them as they sat on their front lawn, two doors down from mine. On our Los Feliz block heavily shaded with cedar trees, the sun peeking through in rays and splotches, they were eating watermelon, juice dripping down their faces and shirts. Grace's hands drenched. She was younger and had an awkward grip on the large fruit. Both of them had the same thick, black hair, tanned skin, and almond shaped eyes. Sam had motioned for me and said, "Stop staring and come get some. There's extra," his voice sounding a lot older than he looked.

I'd laid my bike down carefully, noticed how the flower decals were peeling off the pink frame. I'd reached for the latch on the wooden gate and stopped. The hot August, L.A. sun warmed the sidewalk, my bare feet started to burn.

"You just gonna stand there?" he set one rind down on the grass and picked up another out of a giant stainless-steel bowl. My heart pounded, but I'd shrugged, "No." I opened the gate carefully and sat down across from them. Grace got up, walked over, handed me a piece, barely able to juggle it with her small hands. "You're our first friend," she'd said, her sticky hand resting on my arm. I could see empty moving boxes on the side of the carport. I smiled in response and looked at Sam, seeing if he agreed. He shrugged his shoulders, laid back on the grass and closed his eyes.

Richard comes back in the room and picks up his jacket resting on the back of the couch. "I'll be back in the morning. I'll bring breakfast." He comes over to me, leans down and kisses my forehead. I let my face rub against his—his skin prickly, rough and slicing. The reminder of a man.

Isabelle puts out her cigarette.

Richard pulls out his keys. "Sleep well," he says. He's careful not to intrude, to leave before he's asked to. He extends his hand formally and I take it. I stand up, and give him a hug, my face in his neck and breathe in his smell. Cologne, fall leaves and Shea. The scent mixes with Isabelle's smoke. I suddenly know both of them, again, their scents; it's one of the ways I remember them when they aren't here. I glance over his shoulder. Isabelle's looking away, turning from what she can't or doesn't want to understand.

I look around the dark guestroom closet for a long time. Isabelle comes up behind me and turns on the light and it startles me, stinging my eyes. I'm reminded of two nights ago, my premiere, sitting in the back of the car, the driver flicking on the interior light abruptly, without warning. I had listened to a message on my phone from Russ, his voice panicked. He was stuck in traffic, something about a lane closure on the Sepulveda Pass, his voice pleading, "Don't do anything, wait for me in the car." I'd focused on the back of the driver's head and the crisscross lines on the nape of his neck. I'd counted to three, again and again, but Russ wasn't coming. I put my hand on the door handle that was still so slippery, eventually nudging my shoulder against it to try and open it. My driver told me to stay put, that he'd come around. The door opened, the cold air rushing in and his hand extended to me, and I was afraid to touch it. I tried to get my footing, to find strength in my legs. The blast of lights turned everything white and I told myself to ignore the hum and hysteria of the crowd, to walk the two hundred yards to the theatre, to not blink when the bulbs flashed. My driver guided me into the blocked off the streets of Westwood. People pressed against the barriers, reaching toward us, the massive light fixtures looking like bare trees. Popping sounds bounced everywhere like fireworks being muted by rain. Ryan Gosling stood a few feet away, his hands in his pockets, smiling sweetly as he talked to a reporter, but I heard no sound. My legs were not steady, but my driver withdrew his arm, saying he had to move the car. A squeaky voice of an event assistant sang as her hand grabbed mine, keeping me far away from the press line, but she let go when the first *E! News* reporter jammed a microphone in my face. I'd nodded, tried to focus, the bright pink neon sponsorship signs blurred, making me nauseous. I felt my mouth move, but didn't recognize anything

I said. Seconds later, I heard myself ask if she'd seen my husband and her microphone drooped a little, her caked on smile fell as she took a step back. Her cameraman looked up from the view finder.

Then Russ's hand grabbed my arm, his other sweaty palm stuck to the small of my back, digging in. His eyes opened wider when I said again, louder, "Where's Sam? I have to wait for him." His stern voice instructed the camera man to stop filming and then I felt a smile spreading over my face as I leaned into him and he hurried us the rest of the way down the carpet. Right before entering the doors my head turned to the side, my eye-catching Sam's in the crowd, him lifting his chin, his hair falling away from his face. And then I was inside, being steered down a damp alley into a waiting car. Russ shook his head as he covered me with his suit jacket, saying, "I'm sorry, Evie, I'm sorry, Evie." Again and again, the soft gentle rhythm of his voice.

"Eva," Isabelle says, putting her hand on my arm. I feel jerked from the memory, and I take a step away from her. "Do you need help finding something?" she asks, almost looking afraid.

"I don't recognize anything I own," I tell her, my eyes filling with tears, trying to push the images from the premiere out of my head, the shame overwhelming me, not wanting to picture any more. Not wanting to envision Russ's devastated face in the hospital. His tie loosened around his neck, head hung as Richard spoke to him in a low voice, trying not to blame him, asking him to get to work on damage control.

Isabelle stands still, not sure of what to do or say.

"Did you use this one last time you were here?" I hold out the blanket.

She shakes her head. "There was a random heat wave." She's right. It was humid almost balmy right after Sam died. The air was sticky, the palm trees and wind chimes stopped moving, and the ocean barely had waves.

She won't take it, so I spread it across the bed. "It's fall," I say. "It's going to be cold tonight." I walk over to the window to shut the binds, letting the bedtime rituals distract me and keep me moving.

"What do you want to do in the morning?" Isabelle asks.

She sounds like we're vacationing, like we're staying at a Polynesian style resort on the Kohala coast, the exterior outlined in palm trees, surrounded by gentle waves lapping against lava rocks. Why am I surprised at this? Had I let my guard down, or had I just naturally assumed that like me, everyone had been stripped down to realism. I look at her, study her but see nothing; she's oblivious, with only a calm expression waiting for the answer to a question still lingering in the air.

I stare out the window and focus on the water, its dark shimmer. I'm afraid if I face her, I might tell her to go. Or I'd grab her, force her down in front of the T.V., let her see me, make her watch *Access Hollywood* until she could face who I'd become. Maybe I'll make her google my name and see the comments, the video clip of me reposted countless times.

"Tomorrow I'm picking up Grace from the airport," I say.

"I can do it," she says.

I turn around and she's pulling her pajamas out of her suitcase. "I told her I'd be there," I say.

"Did she ask you to come? I can't imagine she'd expect you to," Isabelle says, taking off her socks.

I shake my head. Her question enters me, feeling like a flat pry bar chipping away at cracking stucco. "Of course, she didn't," I say. I'd insisted on her coming. The idea of spending time alone with Grace was the only thing I thought could get me out of the house. I want to sit next to her, to be reminded of things from our childhood and everything since.

"Are you going to be alright tonight?" Isabelle asks as she buttons the front of her silk nightshirt. She does it with ease, not looking down.

I nod.

"Where'd Richard put your medicine?" she asks, and takes the large clip out of her hair, letting it fall around her shoulders.

"In my bathroom, I think," I answer.

"I never told you how much I like how that bathroom turned out," she says, pulling back the blankets on the bed. "You walk in and you think you're somewhere in Sardinia."

Who cares? I can barely go into that bathroom, see the large glass mosaic tiles and tall calla lilies in wood vases. I have to close my eyes, feel around for what I need. Sam designed it, sketched it on a napkin at Café Noir while waiting for me to come out of a dress fitting in a designer's shop in Soho. His cold drink set on top of it, making the pen ink smear.

I hardly manage a "good night" as Isabelle opens a magazine.

"It won't be that bad," she says, not looking up. "We will get through it."

She's talking about what happened and what will come next, what possibly waits for me outside this house: a mental diagnosis, more medicine, being dropped by my talent agency, never being able to be insured on a film again, or possibly the inability to heal. "What won't be that bad?" I ask, anyway.

She raises her eyebrows, as if the question surprised her. "People will forget. They'll be on to the next story soon enough."

But will they? I've done sixteen films, had co-starred in a few blockbusters. Photographers have taken pictures of me coming out of grocery stores, pushing a full cart in jeans and a black L.A. Dodger hat on slow news days. *TMZ* had posted a few pictures of Sam and me coming out of a Fourth of July party at Streisand's house two years ago. A caption "Can You Get More Beautiful?" over Sam's head.

Maybe she's telling me we've seen worse.

I look at her for a long time, her hair in brown waves across the white pillow, and her nightshirt mis-buttoned. "See you in the morning," I say, slowly heading for the door. There is an empty space next to her on the bed and I feel that child-like pull momentarily—to stay; to crawl under the covers, to know what it is to be protected, to smell the freshness of her lotion, watered wildflowers.

I shut the door, thinking maybe she's right, that people will forget. But I couldn't. I can't. I am endlessly awake, remembering everything.

FOUR

A fork is set down too hard, and I glance across the dinner table at my mother, Richard and Grace. Food is steaming around matching glasses, maroon placemats, glazed terracotta dishes and vanilla ice sunflowers sit in the middle of all of us. I realize that the last time we were all together was at Sam's funeral over a year ago. This makes me want to get up, go, find somewhere bland, colorless, soundless and odorless—a place that won't remind me of anything.

"Eva," my mother says. "What are you thinking?" She cuts her salmon in small pieces and keeps one eye on me. Her hair is pulled back in a low pony tail, the dramatic slick-back accentuating her cheekbones and her gold hoop earrings swing back and forth.

"Eva," Grace says softly, as if she's trying to coax me out of my thoughts or a fog or something.

"Maybe the drive to the airport was too much on her," Isabelle says to Grace, as if I'm not here.

I shake my head but don't say anything. Have they all seen the news yet, have they signed online or has Russ called yet and told them my career is over, or maybe worse, just beginning. Opportunities and offers for sit down interviews on Dateline or 20/20.

"Eva," Isabelle says again, and takes a sip of wine. Her tone feels condescending, like she's speaking to a young child who can't yet grasp big words. I shake my head, still amazed at how young I feel around her. Like I'm five- years- old, waiting for her to pick me up from school, the last one sitting on the steps, eager and desperate with anticipation watching every car that turns into the driveway. I always managed that childlike hope that she'd come, run to the steps, pull me in a hug, lift me and wrap me in her sweater with her gardenia scent and her nurturing away the fear of being left there, abandoned.

"Eva," Isabelle says again.

I want to yell at her, ask her what *she's* doing here, now, after all this time. Where was she was for the months leading up to this? How could she never have known how bad it was for me? I wore the same sweatpants and gray tank top, day after day, that I lost count of the months after Sam died. The blinds remained shut, dark blankets draped over to create total blackness. Sweaty sheets greeted me most mornings, as did ocean salt-stained windows, piles of dishes, mail and messages. Why does she suddenly sit across from me, worried, concerned? Why did she believe me when I told her I was fine when we spoke? Didn't she hear the strain in my voice, or didn't the hollowness of my tone echo over the phone? Is she here now because my warning signs were splashed all over the T.V. and the internet and if she didn't come, people would judge her, point a finger? Was it Richard or Lily that made her come? Ask her the question, how could you not? Why does it always take a big event, wedding, birth, death, or catastrophe to get her to on a plane or to snap-to.

"The drive was fine," I say, trying to remain calm. "I took your rental car. No one noticed me."

"Eva's good," Richard says, winking at me, reassuring. I want him to say it again and again, so I'll believe him. "We're all here," he says. He'd gone home last night and the sleep and shower restored him to the man I know, at least physically. His vintage tee shirt and jeans relax me. Remind me of going to a matinee movie or a Laker game. His quietness, the way he only says things when it's necessary gives a calm, boundary to the table.

Grace nervously cuts her fish, her knife slipping a bit. It's only been a few hours since I picked her up from LAX; her flight from Seattle was early. The long car ride was silent because neither one of us knew what to say, or where to start or what we were to each other now. What was our label? Were we childhood friends still? Were we still considered family even after Sam's death? Instead of letting the quiet consume me, question whether it was a mistake to have her come, I rolled the windows all the way down. The traffic noise, the speed of the car made it too loud to hear each other, anyway. When we'd gotten to the top of a hill on PCH, at the stop light of Civic Center Way, she'd reached over and took my hand and squeezed and I forgot all my questions.

Isabelle sips her wine tilting the glass with two fingers. Her Cartier Love bracelet slides down her slender wrist. Under the table, cotton balls separate her freshly painted toes. Crimson Red, her usual, the color she painted mine the day of Sam's funeral. I wouldn't get up out of bed that morning, so she'd pulled back the blankets and started painting my toes. As tears rolled down my eyes, she tightened her grip on my foot and I saw the brush shaking in her hand. I think the fact that she was trying her best to love me, eventually got me up and dressed.

"Would you like some more wine?" Richard asks everyone, holding up the bottle of Pinot Gris.

His tone is the same as it was when Grace and I arrived, low and patient. When we'd come in, he was sitting on the deck, feet on the railing, mug on his lap, bomber jacket slung over the chair. He kissed my cheek and then Grace's, pulled up two seats and gestured for us to sit. We sat for two hours, he talked, then Grace. I was waiting for the sun to set and just listened to them, wrapped in a shawl, grateful to have voices in my house again.

"More wine would be great," I say and look at my plate. My yellow salmon is almost gone, and for a second my life feels normal. Grace's plate is untouched, greens and rice pushed around. My wine splashes as Richard refills it.

"How's school?" Richard asks Grace as he empties the bottle into his own glass and runs his hand through his hair.

I drink quickly, afraid, guessing that soon someone will bring up my premiere, make me recount it—want me to explain in detail why I was swaying, stumbling as I walked, every few steps, tripping on my dress, asking a reporter about my dead husband or how I'd convince everyone to let me go alone.

"It's going well," Grace says. She holds tight to the stem of her glass. "Very well."

She told me the same thing when I picked her up. She was stiff in her seat and kept glancing sideways at my coat. Sam's coat. I forgot to look in the mirror when I'd dressed, just picked up the black canvas jacket out of habit. The worn fleece lined collar, the big size hanging off me was insulating and protective.

"What is it you're doing again?" Isabelle asks Grace, though she remembers. Grace explained it the last time we were together. We all knew she was in her second year at University of Washington's Institute of Marine Studies, a few months away from becoming a marine biologist.

Richard clears his throat.

"Mainly doing research right now," Grace says.

I want to reach across the table, put my hand over hers, and thank her for coming, for protecting me in small ways. I needed to thank her for the way she didn't speak, just nodded, as if to tell me, it would be okay.

"Research on what?" Isabelle asks.

I look over at my mother. She's asking any question she can think of, grasping, talking around things, around me, topics she cannot face. Her glass is already empty and I guess she's on her way to drunk. Her eyes are squinty and her voice drawn out. I learned very young the signs of adults drinking too much. Especially my mother. Her voice would become softer, inviting, but her body language distant, tense, arms crossed. She'd say phrases like, "I wish I would have," or "It's so easy to make mistakes when you're young."

"Larval rockfish in the Georgia Basin of the Sound," Grace says, shifting in her chair.

"Puget Sound," I say to Isabelle and smile at Grace.

"Yes, I know," Isabelle says quickly.

I'm thinking that if I push her enough, she'll get up, go or even slam her hands down on the table and say something real.

"We're trying to determine where they originate," Grace continues. "Where they are when they go through their dispersal phase."

"It sounds fascinating," Richard says.

Is he getting drunk, too?

Richard puts his elbows on the table. "I like it up there. I toyed with the idea of buying a place in Vancouver."

"That's where I want to go when I graduate," Grace says. "Get a job. Hopefully this time next year."

They look at each other; they've found something in common, finally, Vancouver. It makes sense. The seaport metropolitan, the lights sprinkling lemon drops at nightfall. The outskirts, areas with endless miles of dark sky and glowing green clusters of Douglas Firs. Like the two of them, it's sophisticated, mixed with brightness, mystery, natural depths that appear to take forever to discover.

I sit back a little, feel my neck relax and I listen to her talk about her research.

"I would have made a great marine biologist," Isabelle says and Grace fidgets with her earlobe, turning the black diamond stud. "Remember when you were little, Eva, and I used to spend hours with you on the beach naming all the different sea creatures?"

Richard's eyes are on me, shaking his head, giving me a look as if to say let it go.

"No, I don't," I say to Isabelle. "I have no memory of us doing that." I hear my therapists voice in my head saying it's important not to affirm people's lies. She says powerful people—or those we have given our power to can influence, manipulate, reinvent history in their own self-protection. They'll tell tales of bliss to anyone who will listen, their voices taking us into a state of hypnosis, walking us down a shadowy staircase into vaults of made-up stories. They'll create childhoods filled with hours spent on beaches, sand between toes, building sandcastles that kept being carried away by waves, walks in parks, sticky hands from afternoon ice creams, fresh cookies stuck to plates, splattered art projects and hot breakfasts that never happened. And those of us who remember a different story or version are left feeling robbed of our history: the good and the bad.

"When will you move up to the Islands, you think?" Richard asks Grace. It's not like Richard to ask questions he knows the answer to, so I know despite his groomed appearance, he's exhausted, distracted, that the last two days are starting to get to him, seeping in, cracking that tough exterior that so many of us lean against.

Grace stops fidgeting with her earring and looks at me. "Next year," she says patiently.

A phone rings. No one moves to answer it. Grace smiles and nods at me. A sly grin at first, then slowly it spreads into a broad smile revealing a deep dimple on the left cheek. It is a smile that always makes me think she knows something I don't, the same one she's always had. I first noticed it when I saw her sitting cross-legged, next to her mother in the garden. Both of them dressed in loose pastel skirts, tank tops and faded sun hats. Grace's hair in braids, one slightly longer than the other.

"Do you ever miss Southern California?" Isabelle asks Grace when the phone stops ringing.

"Do you?" I ask Isabelle. The napkin in my hand is wadded up so tight and I squeeze harder.

"Eva," Richard says, setting down his fork.

"No, I don't miss it," Isabelle says, ignoring him.

"I do," Grace says, quietly.

I imagine she's picturing the Los Feliz house where she and Sam lived with their mother, Demetria, for a while. The blue cottage, pale yellow trim and rainbow rose bushes with overgrown fuchsia cover-crops. She always followed her mother around, trailing behind, in and out of the back patio door with a screen that whined and snapped shut always staring and emulating Demetria. I know now, that all those hours, Grace was memorizing her mother because she'd need it later.

"I take that back," Isabelle says. "I miss certain things about this place. Certain people." She stares out at the ocean, not daring to look at Richard or me.

"I know what you mean," Grace says.

CHAPTER

FIVE

Coffee sits in front of me, the twist of black and white steam rising from the cup. I look at everyone at the table, knowing they've watched me eat, relieved with each bite. It's been hours of this. I'd let the conversation carry around me, occasionally giving a nod, a smile they knew and recognized.

"I think I'll excuse myself," I say, wanting to escape before one of them brings up anything about the screening of my movie, *Endlessness*, three nights ago, or the last year. I just want to enjoy them being here and hearing sounds again in a once empty house: dishes banging, different footsteps and newspaper pages turning between bites or sips in the morning.

"We think some time away would be good for you," Isabelle says, looking at me and then Richard.

Richard nods. "Your mother mentioned getting a place in the desert for a while."

Isabelle wraps her hands around her mug. "Marty knows a good doctor down there."

I haven't heard her ex-boyfriend's name in a long time, the tanned golf pro with blond hair and wrinkly knees. I don't want to think that he knows anything about me, or psychiatrists, an intervention, or a plan. It reminds me that along with the rest of the world, Isabelle has access to my life now. If I turn on the computer, there will pictures of me—some gossip blogger having used a white pen and written a caption bubble over my head. It felt like so many people suddenly knew my fears, failures. I was a canvas, wide open for judgment, various narratives painted on me. I have no choice but to stand shamed, bare, waiting for something or somebody to cover me.

Grace stares at her plate, her nails tapping the table.

"I can't get away now," I say. "I have to focus on damage control." I don't even care about movies anymore, but I say it anyway.

"Russ will help handle all that," Richard says and straightens his shoulders. "I talked to him for a while today."

Russ. My manager, most likely in front of his computer, hair slicked back, the gel making it appear darker than it is, trying to compose a statement for the press—a compilation of things, a grieving, sleep-deprived actress, a widow, an almost mother, so please respect privacy at this time.

"He knows you need some space. Some time," Richard says.

Isabelle slides her chair back. "You told me you were taking the next year or two off, anyway. I thought that's what you decided."

"I don't remember what I decided," I say.

"I really think some time away would be good, Eva," Richard says. He looks at me, and I know it's hard for him to say it. They both look at Grace, wanting her to chime in.

Taking in everyone gathered around the table, around me, I hear Dr. Rose say, "It's not perfect, Eva. But they're here." Is this their intervention, attempt to rally, circle in around me, prop me up, dust me off, push me back out the door? Is this the village I always wanted —if I accepted all its limitations and imperfections.

I stare at the massive framed, vintage poster of a bullfighter that Sam insisted we buy when we were in Spain eight years ago. The one he carried, in a brown stained tube, on four different planes and two boats, in order to get it home. He said he bought it to remember where and when we fell in love again, as adults. He'd said souvenirs were important, especially that trip. He'd come to visit Grace and me when I was filming the independent, *Camino Lost*, in Sevilla.

Grace was off from school for the summer and moved into to the rental house I was staying in. She'd convinced Sam and his girlfriend to come visit for a week, hop a plane over from New York. He and Kate had arrived. She was petite and blonde, with bangs that hung over her eyes dramatically, making her large blue eyes look childlike. She fit right under his arm when they walked. After four days of them being there, I'd received a text from Grace when I was on set—that Kate had left, packed a bag and boarded a plane because there had been a huge fight. We'd had a late shoot that went until three a.m. so I'd slept in the trailer not returning to the house until the next night. I'd found Sam in the living room, sitting, leaning back on the cracked leather sofa, his bare feet resting on the coffee table. When I'd entered the door he'd said, "How was work" and "She's gone," in what seemed like one sentence, one breath. I just clung to my purse, not able to set it down or come in the room any further. I had just stood there and allowed myself to remember years ago, as teenagers, making love in the middle of the night on the beach in a protective cove, a Mexican embroidered blanket on the sand, my hair fanned out, his hand supporting the small of my back so my skin wouldn't rub raw, speaking Spanish as he moved inside me, not even realizing he was going in and out of languages.

"Why'd you come here," I'd said to him, noticing no lamps or lights were on.

He'd looked at me and said, "To make sure you and Grace were good." He'd stood up and I took a step back—an immediate reaction to his movement.

"Why'd Kate leave," I had whispered.

"She thinks I'm in with love you," he stared straight ahead, and crossed his arms.

I hugged my purse across my chest and said, "How could you love me. You disappeared, dropped off the face of the earth. No word from you for three years."

He took another step closer towards me and put his hands in his pockets. I focused on the hole in the knee of his jeans.

"Look at me," he said.

I knew I couldn't. I knew if I looked at him, I would see the little boy waiting for his mother on the front steps to come back from chemo treatments, his knees skinned, his feet on a skateboard rolling it back and forth.

It was quiet for a long time. "Maybe you should go, too," I'd said looking at the corner of the coffee table. I knew if he touched me, I wouldn't be able to turn away.

He shook his head, taking a few more steps and stopping. "I shouldn't have disappeared," he said. "I couldn't think clearly anymore. Your career was taking off, you were never around. And what did I have?"

"And now," I said, not taking a second to think about what he was saying, admitting. I didn't even recognize the tone of my own voice. It was higher pitched.

"It's different," he said, shifting his weight.

I finally looked up, met his gaze and then I studied the tattoos on his arms that peeked from just below the sleeves of his white tee shirt. I couldn't make out what they were of, just that they were recent and very black.

I stood still as he crossed the rest of the way to me, letting his words, "it's different" ring in my head, not knowing what to believe, allowing myself to feel the hope in the words. He reached out, lifted my chin and then pulled me to him, kissed me. He took the purse from my arms and set it down and then backed me up towards the window. The light coming through and he looked different than I'd seen him, his face carved out, stubble growing on his cheeks, and chin, his eyes scared. "Okay," I said, before I could stop myself. He lifted my tank top and pushed back my shoulders. Everything becoming suddenly frantic, urgent and I couldn't stop. My breasts arched, hair falling back and then forward. Blue light coming through the curtains—his skin looked dark and then white. He pulled at my skirt and underwear and I stepped out of them. His mouth bit mine and I cried out. His hand covered my lips and I felt my breath, my tongue tracing his fingers. The breeze climbed up my back as he lifted me, my legs wrapping around his waist. He stumbled forward until my back hit the wall. Cold paint, his rough jeans cutting lines in my thighs. He thrusted me higher. I clung onto him, and pulled at his hair until his hair slid back and I could see his eyes. Older, better. A mixture of a laugh and moan escaped one of us or both of us and he fumbled with his buttons. My head in the palm of his hand and I felt him move his face away until it was shadowed.

"Look at me," he said.

And when I did, he pushed himself inside.

"You're right," I say to Isabelle. "Going to a new place might be good." I have to force myself to look away from the painting of the bullfighter carried on a crowd's shoulders. There's too much of Sam here. Too much of what almost was and never was, too much of the good and the bad.

"I could probably get away with you for a while," Grace says.

I lean closer because I can barely hear her. She turns and starts to speak, then stops when she sees I'm still looking at the picture. Her eyebrows crease and she takes a quick breath, like she's trying to stop a sob. Her expression makes me want to cry, for my coffee to spill brown against the taupe linens, for everybody to see what I feel like inside.

I nod. "I'll think about it, Gracie."

"I can only stay here until Sunday," Grace says. "I need to get home and finish up some things."

I'm suddenly jealous that she has a life that keeps her moving, one that she can escape to. Or maybe I'm jealous of her resilience. "That works," I say.

"Why don't you go up north with Grace for a while," Richard says, lowering his voice, though Isabelle has excused herself for a cigarette. "You girls could get a place in the San Juan's.'"

I picture a house on the verge of water, a dock in front, crisp Douglas Firs framing a view of the Cascades.

"I could see if the house you used to stay in is available," Richard says.

I want to look at Grace, but can't. All these places, houses of our childhood, our past and present—houses that bring people back to life.

"Let's do it," I say. "But a different house."

"Do you want me to handle the arrangements?" Richard asks.

I nod, meeting Richard's glance. "Will you come?"

He holds my gaze. "I will try."

"A different house," Grace says, firmly. "I don't want to go back to that one."

The house she, Sam and I spent two summers in as kids after Demetria died—the weathered bungalow with light gray and blue trim, pale walls, white patched quilts on white beds. Dinners at the pizzeria, Grace falling asleep on the car rides home. Her father, Carl, lifting her from the back seat, while holding the groceries. Sam and I walking behind, eleven years old but a little afraid of the dark. Our hands touched as we stared at Carl's bulky shoulders, Grace's arms swinging down his back. Her cheek lay against his long black hair.

I nod, again. "I agree. A new house."

Richard set a hand on the table. "Done." He's most comfortable in this position. Arranging, dictating, and creating.

"I think it'll be good," Grace says.

Does she remember how we felt up there? That even though Carl took us to get away because Demetria died, we still ran, fished, played. That her dad told us we just had to wait, and we would heal. That it worked for a while. With the smell of pines, seawater and a dense fog at sunset—how could we think of death? We were children there.

CHAPTER

SIX

I walk down the stretch of beach in front of my house and wonder if I loved Isabelle too late—or what it would be like to have all those years back, the years spent fighting because we loved differently. We screamed at things we didn't understand, at each other, at my father's absence, running circles around our similarities. It never helped that our eyes, the same color, more yellow than brown, lit with the identical anger when we argued.

I think back to the moment I decided to love Isabelle, or rather admit my love. Right after Sam and I were married. My admission never changed who she was, it changed who I was. Once I let myself love her, I felt a family growing, heard more than two plates being set on a dark wood table at holidays. And then I learned what the risk was for me—loving many people at once. Sam and Isabelle. I loved them when I didn't want to, when it stopped being good for me. Two people, who at times I suspected, if I let them, would swallow me.

Of the two, only one is left.

I wince as cold water washes over my feet and have no idea how long I've been walking, my morning ritual for the last few weeks. I check my watch, it's nine o'clock. I'm relieved I have some time, an hour until I need to leave for my appointment with Dr. Rose. I feel lucky to have found her, that Richard's producing partner had recommended her, said she could be trusted, that she'd saved his marriage. She had a lot of experience with high-profile people, and was quoted throughout medical journals, even though you'd never know it. She had no awards, diplomas or pictures on her walls. Just a wall lined with books written by other people in an office that smelled like toasted wheat bread.

After my last appointment, and at her suggestion, I invited Isabelle. She's probably already dressed waiting for me, or busy worrying what to wear, attempting to look her best, her version of a concerned, conservative, visiting-from-a-major–Metropolitan-city-mother. Tight black pencil skirt, Louboutin heels, an off-white blazer maybe. I look at my outfit, baggy pants rolled up to my calves and a hooded sweatshirt. No one can see the shape of my body, how thin I've gotten and I like it that way. I've grown used to it. For the last month, ever since the premiere, I've practiced hiding myself.

I stand in the ocean, my feet in gushy sand, the rush of water slapping against my ankles. I wonder how long I can stand the cold water; how the frozen feeling reminds me of the way I was living until the premiere.

The gray sky has turned the water a murky ash. A thick fog dampens my clothes and hair. I like the strong smell—burnt algae and salt. I think of Grace in Seattle, how she must smell something similar. Grace, who I imagine is standing knee deep in some part of the Puget Sound, wearing old, battered, olive waders and a big yellow jacket, her research team all around her. Her ponytail loose.

I don't bother to wash the sand off my feet as I climb the coarse wood steps to the house. Taking one last glance at the water and coastline, I know some part of me will miss it when I go. This city is far enough from L.A., hidden from most the photographers in white vans, or darting black cars, far enough removed from the 24 hour drive-thrus, crowds of people walking past. Its innocent, secluded coast sometimes seems so quiet I have to remind myself twelve thousand people live with me. All around me, houses are filled with couples waking up in bed together, limbs and blankets intertwined, coffee gurgling on, the sound of front doors opening, husbands bending down to pick up the *Los Angeles Times*, shaking the morning dew off the plastic cover. Some rituals and routines are already in motion: packing lunch boxes; different size footsteps pacing back and forth on wood floors; refrigerator doors opening and shutting; kids searching for backpacks; jackets half on, cramming in SUVs to rush to school before the bell. They're all things I thought would be a part of my life by now. Instead, my solitude comforts me, makes my days predictable, simple, helping me not to long for other things, for more or for less.

I open the door, pause, for any signs of Isabelle, perhaps a cigarette lighter clicking on or her high heels coming down wood stairs or remnants of almond rose perfume trailing through the kitchen. There's nothing, so I hurry through the living room, for a moment relieved, expecting to see suitcases lined by the door. The same thought I have each time I come in and don't hear or see traces of my mother.

"It makes the drive harder if you go slower than the speed limit," I say.

Isabelle grips the steering wheel as she drives us through Malibu Canyon. "I'm going the speed limit." She glances in the rearview mirror, "I'm not used to all these cliffs and mountains," she says. "It's been a while."

She's right it has been a while—for a lot of things. Being here, spending time with one another. It feels familiar, like we've come full circle from where we began all those years ago in Malibu. Holed up in a house on the sand, haunted by the absence of a man and the things he left behind.

"There's a line of cars behind you," I say. I'm pressing her.

"I am going the speed limit."

She's telling me she's doing her best. I try not to laugh. She is doing her best, maybe even driving slower because of where we're headed. She probably hasn't been to a psychiatrist since my father left—when she'd stomped out in the second session, a fuzzy Chanel maroon coat trailing behind her, leaving me to pick up her purse and find my way to the car.

"I could have driven," I say.

"Not a good idea," she answers.

She still thinks I'm fragile, breakable. "Do you remember the last time we drove through here?"

She places her hands closer together on the top of the steering wheel. "How about some music," she says, reaching to touch the screen on the center console.

"It was right before my wedding," I say. Almost four years ago. It was a cold winter, fog blanketing the canyon roads. It was December. Isabelle had bought a cream, faux fur jacket for me to wear over my strapless wedding dress that buttoned into a V in the front, still showing off the mantilla lace. She'd ordered extra heaters for the backyard of our friend's property. There was a windy path lit by endless floor lanterns, through olive trees to a gazebo style wedding arch made of vine maple branches. Sam stood still as I rounded the corner and our eyes met. As I got closer to him, he shifted his weight and clasped his hands. I started to hear an instrumental version of Leonard Cohen's "Hallelujah" getting louder. Sam's hair was longer, reaching past the collar of his navy suit. When I stopped right at the altar's edge, the string lights elegantly woven through, casting a pastel glow, Sam, had taken a few steps towards me and reached out his hand. When I took it, instead of it being warm like I'd imagined, moist, it was a jolt of cold.

Isabelle slides closer to the wheel and I wait for her to say something.

"We were going to make sure the flowers were right," I say, reminding her.

She shakes her head. I've always loved her profile, I used to trace it with my finger when I was young and she'd fallen asleep reading me a book. Perfect slopes and angles.

"You said the canyon looked like someone smeared gray chalk," I say. I look out the window, the mountains layered around us; the river below is flowing faster than I remembered. "The sun was setting, hitting our eyes. We could barely see."

"I don't remember that," she says.

"I remember," I say. "I liked that day."

I know she remembers. I think she believes if she denies all my memories, then maybe, I will heal.

Isabelle sticks close to me as we walk inside, our sleeves brush every few steps. The run-down wood paneled building is heavily shaded with an overhang of drooping trees. Just as she's about to say something about it, or criticize my choice in a doctor, I remind her of the reason Dr. Rose chose to meet here, in the valley. She borrowed an office from a colleague, I tell her, again. She felt it would be detrimental if our whereabouts got out. Her regular office is in Santa Monica, just off Montana Avenue, I tell her. She says people are always looking for people in Santa Monica, waiting to hear things about people in Santa Monica.

As we get in the elevator, I feel nervous. I think of all the times I've walked into new places with my mother, my nerves making me sick: the first day of kindergarten, a mirrored hair salon in New York, an airplane ride, an audition. Only I'm taller now, and I no longer fit in the curve of her hip; my head can no longer rest comfortably on her shoulder.

It's warm and I unbutton Sam's jacket. We get off the elevator, and walk the long hallway, past a vacant pharmacy with the bars pulled down. When we hear voices coming, I turn away, and Isabelle's in front of me. She's protecting me, shielding me from recognition.

Five minutes later, Dr. Rose opens the waiting room door and pauses. She says hello, a little startled, as if she's surprised to find us there. Her eyes linger on Isabelle and she tries not to stare. It's a look I recognize, reminding me again that my mother stuns people, even more so as she's softened by age, her confidence more noticeable. Isabelle looks back at Rose and does a once over of her own.

I stand up and make the introductions. Dr. Rose crosses to Isabelle, who remains seated. They shake hands and for a second, I feel sorry for my mother. Is she not getting up because she's scared?

Is the thought of walking through this door and into the office suddenly too intimidating? Was it too much to ask her to come here? Face someone who already knows about her, all the mistakes she's made? She was never given the opportunity to unveil herself, tell her narrative, her side. Does she worry that I've only painted her in the darkest colors, unfairly at times, or worse, that I painted her fairly and she still fell short? I hold my hand out to her. She ignores it and gracefully rises and shakes Dr. Roses's hand, her hair falling behind her shoulders. She follows a few steps behind me and we settle into a couch with a light grey linen slip color. I tuck a striped pastel pillow under my arm.

"I apologize for the office," Dr. Rose says. She crosses her legs and digs the heel into the carpet. "I'm sure Eva explained. I use this office sometimes when I have patients who want more privacy." Her blue eyes look at Isabelle and then me, and she nods with encouragement.

I lean back further into the pillows and situate myself in. We're sitting in a perfect triangle. I'm at one end of the couch, Isabelle at another and Dr. Rose faces us in a taupe swivel chair. She picks up a water bottle sitting on a chipped end table and takes a sip. Her eyes stay on us, waiting, or giving us a chance to adjust.

"How's your week going," she starts.

"Okay," I say quickly and I feel Isabelle shift and the couch cushions move. Her face is still, her red lips pressed together.

"What's been happening?" Rose asks me. Her questions have a rhythm to them, they're familiar; they walk me in to the session naturally. She gives me the control, lets me lead us into whatever unravels, or the place I need to go.

"Not much has happened," I answer. Isabelle folds her hands in her lap, her maroon nail polish darkening against her black skirt.

"Did you do some of the things we talked about? The goals for this week?" she asks and scribbles something in the leather notebook that rests on her lap.

I nod. "I wrote a little, found the spot on San Juan Island I want to go, I painted some. I left the house a few times for walks." I cringe at how simple it sounds. A life of leisure and luxury. But it felt like the opposite. The easiest most mundane things feel like a row of steep mountains. Each one higher than the one before it.

Isabelle crosses her legs and then uncrosses them. "What sorts of things did you tell her to do?" she asks. The question felt like it was flung through the air.

"Since Eva has started coming regularly, I suggested she set little goals for herself every day," Dr. Rose says, setting down her pen, unfazed by Isabelle's sharp tone and tense body language. "Do things that tap into her creativity. Since she's not acting right now, I thought getting into other artistic medians, writing, painting, would allow her to channel, alleviate the fixation on negative thoughts or images."

"Arts and crafts," Isabelle says.

I look away, rolling my eyes. She's starting I tell myself. "I like it," I say, my tone defensive, feeling protective of Dr. Rose.

"What we're talking about here, Isabelle, is behavior activation," Rose says. "We find things that the patient values and finds rewarding. Whether meeting with friends, exercising, spending time with animals, doing creative projects. The patient takes control, sets goals that she can complete outside our sessions. It's also a way of avoiding things that remind them of their trauma. It's learning how to cope again." She taps her foot slightly and I can't tell if she's irritated.

Isabelle doesn't say anything.

"Eva, why don't you talk more about your reaction to your mom's comment," Dr. Rose continues. "You became visibly annoyed."

Her suggestion startles me. Does she know what she's asking? Doesn't she remember that we don't have that kind of relationship, that I wouldn't know where to begin? Isabelle won't understand. Dr. Rose nods at me, she smiles, the lines around her eyes spreading into what looks like perfect rays.

I take a breath. "Her arts and crafts comment. It felt demeaning."

"That's what it sounded like to me," Isabelle snaps back. She smooths the hair that sweeps across her forehead and stares at Dr. Rose, straight on.

I shake my head at Dr. Rose, pleading her to stop. It's easier just to stay where we are in the relationship, where we've always been. On the edge of the pool, both of us looking over, afraid of the deep end. The shallow part much more comfortable, where the water is lighter, the sun heats it faster, your legs touching the ground to steady you—you can easily pull yourself out.

"I just want to make sure we're on the same page here," Rose says looking back at my mother. "Your daughter is depressed, and at times, has been in despair, which is a terrifying place to be." She pauses for a moment, as if collecting her thoughts, choosing her words carefully. She shifts in her seat. "I'm trying to help her get back to herself, or a place she can begin to function comfortably through small steps, setting routines, pushing herself a little further each day."

Isabelle nods. "I understand she's depressed or has been." Her voice is softer. "I guess what I want to know is why none of these small steps were put into place before all this happened?" Isabelle sniffs loudly.

"You're referring to what happened at her film premiere and leading up to it, correct?" Rose asks, leaning forward.

I feel myself starting to play with my shirt, rubbing the material through my fingers. A tightness in my chest settles around my ribs.

"Eva was in therapy, coming to me some, but not consistently," Rose says. "She wasn't disclosing much. There were a lot of times she didn't show, canceled, wasn't rescheduling."

I nod, agreeing.

"I never saw signs she was a danger to herself. She's strong. I knew she would start coming when she was ready."

I look down, the shame overwhelming me.

"Were you prescribing her meds?" Isabelle asks.

She nods. "A small, controlled dose to help with the anxiety, to help her cope. But it doesn't touch the healing process." She looks at me suddenly, as if she'd forgotten I was in the room, lost in her defense or our defense. She smiles at me, tucks her hair behind her ear.

Isabelle makes a gesture with her hand, as if she's swatting a bug away. "I told myself I wouldn't get involved in any of this," she says and looks at the door.

"Then don't," I say, not able to control the anger in my voice.

She ignores what I say, but addresses me directly for the first time. "I think Dr. Rose should have seen there was a bigger problem than you were letting on. You were obviously fooling her. And us. A lot of embarrassment could have been avoided."

I take a deep breath, pivot so I can look at her. "Whose embarrassment are we talking about?"

She looks at me, but doesn't answer.

Dr. Rose leans back in her chair. "Isabelle, are we talking about the embarrassment that Eva feels after the premiere. Or the embarrassment you feel?"

I feel numb, all my defenses returning, shielding myself from her comments, her inability to empathize. I focus on the clock on the bookshelf, noticing for the first time that it makes a faint ticking noise. "Are you going to answer," I ask her, my gaze on the clock. I feel myself reaching out to touch her arm. She pulls it away before I can reach her.

"No," she says finally.

I inch closer to the edge of the couch and look at Dr. Rose, wondering if there's anything she can do.

"I think it's important that we stay here, on this topic," Rose says, urging us, her tone soft, maybe realizing, this is where Isabelle and I get stuck right in the middle of the pool, the part that begins to slope, right before the drop-off into the deep end.

Isabelle tucks her hair behind her ears, her hand trembles a little. I've rarely seen her do this—she has always thought her ears stick out too much, she told me once she was teased endlessly in the third grade.

"Do you want to say something, Eva," Rose asks. She's nudging me, almost walking me, hand in hand, showing me that we all have the tools, the limbs and ability to push off, into the deep part of the water.

I hug the throw pillow tightly to me. I look down at it, focus on the striped pattern. I feel like I'm choking the words out. "I feel like that's all that mattered to you. The embarrassment of it all."

"Don't be ridiculous," Isabelle says quickly. Her voice is monotone. It feels like she's pulling further and further away, our time together these last weeks, and the rhythm and comfort we were building, waning.

I focus on Dr. Rose's slingback heels, the black leather on the pointed part starting to peel away.

Isabelle leans back, lets out a breath. "I think you misunderstood me," she says to Dr. Rose. "What I meant was I wanted to know why you didn't pick up on her mental state. Why the whole thing wasn't prevented?"

"I understand," I say softly, feeling myself relax a little, feeling her coming back, trying a little.

"Eva wasn't communicating a lot during that time, how she was feeling, what she feared. She was presenting a different image to me. To everyone."

"She's right," I say, suddenly feeling so protective of her. "It wasn't her fault, wasn't anyone's fault. It was easy for me to do. Mask it. Pretending, becoming someone else is like breathing for me."

"I just can't imagine that if a person is seeing or talking to a dead person, they hide it from everyone around them." She sits up straighter, stares straight ahead, past Dr. Rose.

"You can say his name," I say.

They both look at me.

"Are you worried or feeling guilty that you should have seen it to?" Rose asks her.

Isabelle looks down at her hands and in a barely audible whisper says, "No."

"It's not anyone's fault," I say again. "I hid things for a long time. How bad it had gotten. It's easy for me to do. It's my job. Was my job."

"Why did you?" Isabelle asks. She's suddenly almost childlike, the way she hangs her head and starts to look up and then immediately looks down again. I can imagine her as a child, even though there's hardly any pictures of her. Most everything burned in a fire when she was fifteen. But I can see how she was, her pale brown eyes peering from behind pale blonde bangs that needed to be trimmed, her ears poking out of her short hair.

"That's what we're working on," Rose says. "Breaking patterns. Once Eva's able to say that aloud, release it. That's the place we can really start to do some work." She sets down the pen that she's been holding. "You being here is very important."

"I've known," Isabelle says, looking out the window. "That she hides her feelings."

Dr. Rose studies us. She nods and I think, how could my mother not know that about me. She taught me about disguising, covering, opening your eyes wider to stop approaching tears. I watched her.

Rose watches us, studying. She nods at me again, and I remember that I've come to trust her. She's the only person I've been honest with since Sam died.

Dr. Rose uncrosses her legs and then crosses them again. "I also want you to know how hard it's going to be for Eva. The road ahead. She needs to feel safe, and have a support system."

"I know," Isabelle says, her voice defensive. She outlines her knee-cap with her nail.

"The road ahead?" I ask her, suddenly so afraid of it.

"The healing process," she answers. "You've experienced two losses in a short period of time."

I close my eyes, it's the first time I've heard someone say it in a long time, heard anyone reference my miscarriage. I'd forgotten she knew, that I'd uttered it one afternoon to her because I thought it would release some pressure I felt permanently on my chest. Maybe if I told her, it would make everything hurt less, maybe ease and soften the harshness of losing the baby weeks after he died.

"What we've witnessed with Eva is post-traumatic stress," Dr. Rose continues. Her gaze is locked on Isabelle, forcing her to listen. "What she experienced with PTSD, the debilitation, the disconnect, a depression developed. I didn't treat her before but I'm supposing there might have been past depression, a history that just deepened the intensity."

They both turn to me, and I don't know what I'm supposed to say. I look down, study my hands, trying to focus on what Rose just said, afraid if I try to answer or look up at them, I will see pity on their face. I'd never heard that diagnosis before, the technical, medical terms and it makes me feel better for a moment. Things diagnosed, can start to be treated. There's a hope of healing, a recovery. Isabelle reaches over and puts her hand on top of mine. Her long, beautiful fingers fold around mine and there's a warmness that spreads as her grip gets tighter. The touch, the contact, is jarring, so unexpected. I stop myself before I instinctually jerk away. I feel the tears sliding down my face, and in the safeness of this office with a watery blue glow, I close my eyes and let myself remember what I haven't been able to: Sam's funeral. I see the boat, the minister, and the cracked gray fishing trawler passing only yards away. My dress was too tight. Nausea bobbed up and down between my stomach and throat. Richard's hands surrounded my waist, propping me up, his oversized wool coat over my shoulders, my face caked in Isabelle's Dior make up. Grace on the bow not turning around as the minister spoke. Her black, silk chiffon skirt fanning out behind her as the wind picked up, revealing a snag in her tights where she slipped stepping on board. Isabelle glanced at me every few seconds, holding the white roses as if they were a child, nervous, attentive, waiting for her cue to throw them overboard with the ashes.

"Eva," Rose says. She gets up and grabs a box of Kleenex and hands it to me. She rests her hand on my shoulder for only for a moment before sitting back down. "What are you thinking about?" she asks as she sits back down.

"Things," I say, wiping my eyes. I can picture Sam's ashes drifting away, settling onto the water's surface, the gray quickly turning into a dark, navy blue. I watched them until they vanished thinking I would never believe the autopsy report—that he was killed by sudden impact, multiple blunt force trauma while traveling northbound on his chromed Harley Davidson V-Rod up by Oxnard. I believed the coroner put that as a formality. It was his unhappiness that killed him.

I finally look up, Isabelle's grip loosens on my hand as her palm starts to moisten. Dr. Rose scoots to the edge of her chair, the signal that our time is up. "Isabelle, would you be willing to come a few more times before you leave? I think we made some real headway here today."

My mother turns to me, maybe wondering if it's all worth it, or if she can do it. And then what seems like minutes later, she nods to Dr. Rose.

❧

As we drive back home, there's silence something Dr. Rose refers to as processing, or avoidance. It's probably a little of both. I lean back in the passenger seat and think about what Rose said right before we left. Just as Isabelle walked out of the office ahead of me, Rose took both my hands and said she was proud of me. And when I started to turn away, she squeezed them and said, "In order to mourn Sam's death the right way, you need to mourn the state of the relationship first. Your part in it. Your share." When I nodded, pretending I understood exactly what she meant, she released my hands. I turned and there was Isabelle standing just outside the doorway watching us. When she realized I saw her, she quickly looked up at the ceiling, her hair falling away from her face.

Isabelle turns off the radio and I believe that even though she can't say it, she understood what Dr. Rose was referring to. That I loved Sam the way she loved my father with no exceptions, with all his faults, never questioning, taking anything we could get. The only way it would end, is if they left first.

"Do you need anything from the store?" she asks, tapping her finger nails on the steering wheel.

"Not that I can think of."

"I'll go straight home, then."

"Ok." I'm having trouble getting the simple words out, still not really believing everything that just happened in the office. The connection, the memories flooding back, her taking my hand, the cozy insulation that room provided and the impossible transition of stepping outside, back into the cold.

"Aren't you hungry?"

I smile. She sounds awkwardly maternal.

I shake my head. I know I'm supposed to watch my nutrition, have greens, antioxidants and food with colors—that it's part of healing. When was the last time I ate? My stomach has felt so contracted, the muscles clamping up with nerves, there always seems to be no room, the panic resting where the food's supposed to be.

Isabelle slows and stops the car at the traffic light and glances in the rearview mirror. "I'm thinking about staying another month or two," she says nonchalantly, as if she just told me she drank the last of the rose'.

I pull at my seat belt to adjust it because it feels tight. "I'm thinking about driving up to meet Grace soon," I say. "To Seattle."

I wait for her to let out a deep breath and puff out her lips or for her shoulders to tense, the right side higher than the left, the way she does when something is unacceptable to her.

"I want to drive, instead of fly. I want the privacy, don't want to deal with people. And I need time by myself," I say before she can get a word in. Over a month has gone by with us in the same house. My house. Taking care of each other in small ways, another blanket, setting the coffee timer, tip-toeing around each other awkwardly, like familiar strangers who know each other's habits but not what they're thinking or about to say.

"I don't think it's a good idea for you to go yet," Isabelle says. She accelerates at the green light, turns onto PCH. The sun has just disappeared, leaving smeared lines of yellow, soft pink and violet settling perfect layers above the horizon.

"I've been thinking a lot about it," I say. "Going in a couple weeks."

She doesn't respond, instead she clasps both hands on top of the wheel. I sink even deeper in the seat.

"You're an adult. I just hope you continue the therapy," she says.

"I plan to," I say quickly. "Rose said we can have a weekly or bi-weekly Zoom appointments. Or whatever I need. She's getting some referrals for up there, too, just in case."

She shrugs her shoulders, as if she's surrendered.

I see the turn-off ahead to my house, the curve of the coastline and the sapphire light glowing off the cove. I worry for a second that I am now doing what she, Sam and others had always done to me. Just when things were getting better between us, softening, yielding, just when the door was opening, I am the breeze that closes it.

CHAPTER
SEVEN

When I woke up this morning, I'd laid out two pairs of sweatpants, three pairs of jeans, one dress, tall motorcycle boots I've had since I was 22, running shoes and Sam's sheepskin collared jacket. Now, there are all sorts of sweaters, shirts, and dresses folded in neat colorful piles on the bed—Isabelle's doing. In her mind, all puffy, warm clothes for a cold, damp winter on an island off the coast of Washington. My minimalist packing forced aside. I reach for one of the stacks, to start putting things back, but stop. Her quiet, maternal-like gesture gets to me. She means well. And the gestures come so unexpectedly, sporadically, making me realize that I should listen, accept them as signs when they do. Like running into someone coming out of a Starbucks, someone you'd dreamed about the night before, or being handed a Psalms verse printed on a creased index card, on a crowded street corner on a day you feel like giving up.

The house is quiet for the first time since Isabelle came to stay. For the past two months, there has been a steady hum, or some variation of noise: a blender groaning, background music heard faintly between crashing waves, knocks on doors, voices asking, are you okay or do you need anything.

I set my running shoes in my suitcase and realize the truth is I haven't needed anything in a while. Isabelle and Lily have been here, hovering, each in her own way. Lily would check on me hourly, poking her head in my bedroom, cleaning the sun deck every time I lay out there reading. Isabelle would tiptoe the halls, attempting to figure out which room I was in, leaning over the balcony railing trying to spot me as I come in from a beach walk. Both of them at one time or another, handing me plates of food, books on grief, on loss, on starting over, trays of home-cooked bulging desserts, bouquets of flowers to brighten up rooms. Asking to watch a new movie or series. Each time I did, I tried to get up before the credits started rolling—bringing a long a question I couldn't answer. Would I ever see my name drifting across a black screen again.

The only time I felt truly relaxed was when Richard visited. He never asked what I needed, he would just say, "You feel like walking on the beach? How about a movie?" Other days, we'd sit on the balcony and he'd tell me about his show in pre-production, or we'd discuss the tides, the weather, how the only good thing about the recent Santa Ana winds were the peach sunsets. And when I didn't feel like talking anymore, he would know. He'd let the conversation taper off, lean back in his chair and pretend to be captivated by the ocean—as if he'd found something so incredible, he needed silence to appreciate it.

I have two bags. I don't know how long I'll stay on San Juan, or if I'll stay. I would prefer to take one suitcase, filled with all my comfort clothes and buy anything else I needed. But I see Isabelle and Lily's faces, the worry they can't disguise. Somehow multiple bags make them feel like I will be okay.

Lily helps me carry stuff downstairs. She takes the largest suitcases, careful not to nick the walls as she struggles down the hall and then the staircase. As I get to the kitchen, I see Isabelle's things already lined up at the door. A matching set of Louis Vuitton luggage, a red leather carry-on most likely stuffed with magazines from my coffee table, a make-up case with glossy tubes, and an opened bag of black licorice she swears she doesn't eat.

I had to hand it to Isabelle. She stayed in Malibu longer than I thought.

We still have three hours until our planes leave. She'd insisted on scheduling her flight back to New York as close to my Seattle departure as possible. For convenience, Eva, she'd said, or something like that. The synchronizing had more to do with her and how she'd got so used to not leaving me alone. Or maybe she thought I wouldn't get on the plane if I wasn't escorted—that I'd disappear, drive aimlessly, forget to stop for gas, end up living on a park bench or under one.

"Did you see the email from Richard?" Isabelle says and I turn surprised because I didn't see her. She's sitting in the sofa chair in the front room, her gaze on the ocean.

"I didn't see it," I say.

I look at my phone, open the email and see a picture of a sprawling bungalow—style home surrounded by trees. A long dock in front and two boats tied up. I read the fine print: *Home built by the sea. A mystical, 2 story custom waterfront retreat on the north end of the Island. Sounds of waves, panoramic views, nature and wildlife right outside your windows. Three bedrooms, three bath with den, expansive decks and deep water dock. Twenty-to-Thirty-minute drive to town.*

"The house looks decent," she says.

"It's perfect," I say, scrolling through the rest of the attachments —a flight itinerary, directions to the house, a copy of the lease, and a message: *Place is up for sale. Great Investment.*

"Does Grace have your itinerary?" Isabelle says. "And I arranged for a greeter to also meet you at the other end, in Seattle."

"Thank you," I say again, because she has mentioned it so many times before. I take a deep breath. "Grace is picking me up and we're driving her car up there," I say.

She sets down her glass of water.

"Are you sure you don't want to come?" I ask even though I had willingly accepted her, *no*, weeks ago. I think even Richard urged her to go with us and Lily may have even sat her down and showed her the brochures when they thought I was sleeping. I'm convinced she just wanted to be asked again and again in different settings, different ways, by different people.

She doesn't turn to look at me. I glance out the sliding doors but can't tell what she's looking at. "I'm sure," she says. "I feel better about it now that Dr. Rose cleared it."

I nod. "I have the name of the doctor up there," I say. "And Dr. Rose and I agreed on weekly Zoom sessions."

She leans her head back. "Does Grace still drive the Land Cruiser you bought her? So you guys will be in a safe car . . . "

I nod and grip the counter, "What are you staring at out there?" I ask.

"You and Sam were always generous with her," Isabelle says, looking my way, but not meeting my eyes.

I take a deep breath and try to ignore the comment, heavy with so much innuendo and judgments.

She shrugs when I don't answer and I wonder if it's easier for her to try and pick a fight than say goodbye.

The way she doesn't look at me, the way her bags are lined up at the door—I can't help but think about when she left to move to New York years ago. Her suitcases arranged then exactly as they are now. Largest to smallest, the bags today are flashier and a more expensive brand.

"I haven't been happy here for a while," she had said that day, fifteen years ago, as we stood in the foyer of our Los Feliz house. I'd just come in the door clutching shopping bags, the frozen stuff starting to melt. I didn't want to think about what was in front of me, so I took a deep breath and concentrated on the smell in the room, and wafts of plumeria drifting in from the garden.

"Does Will know you're leaving?" I'd asked, referring to her latest boyfriend. It was all I could think of to say, still in shock.

She looked down at her bags. "He suspects it."

I wanted to tell her I'd been waiting for this day since I was five. Right after my father left, I used to catch her watching me sleep, and there was a time I was convinced, afraid she was memorizing me in case she needed the visual for later. She'd whisper she was going out for errands or to meet someone for a drink. I'd try and wait up for her to come back, pinch my face to keep awake, turn up the late-night cartoons, but eventually I'd fall back asleep. Then, I'd wake in a panic at three or four in the morning, tiptoe down the hall to see if she was in her room, her dark hair fanned across white linens. When she wasn't, I'd return to my bedroom, sit cross-legged on the Moroccan chest at the foot of my bed, my hands placed perfectly in my lap until I heard the garage moan open. I'd crawl under the covers and tell myself that as long as she was home, I could finally sleep.

Isabelle had moved a bag closer to the door with her foot and the foyer was getting darker. I tried not to cry, afraid to admit I thought I was too young not to have any family around, I was days away from celebrating my twentieth birthday, my career was just starting to take off. "Are you going to tell Richard?" my voice insinuating, how could you not? After all he's done for us: visiting us, making sure we were alright, staying a friend to her after two dates that never amounted to anything romantic, making sure we had groceries, jobs, and enough money.

"You can tell him," she'd said.

I studied her outfit. A tailored suit, black turtleneck, knee—high boots, her hair just blown dry and straight. Why was she doing this now? Why couldn't she have gone even a few days ago, when I was still on location, wrapping up the film? Why did she have to wait until I got back, until I'd unpacked, excited to have three months off until my next project? Did she want me to watch her go?

"Were you going to tell me?" I asked.

"You've been busy and not around. A lot's been happening and I knew you needed to concentrate on wrapping."

I'd known her and Will were fighting, I could tell when I had called her.

"How long will you be gone?" I asked.

"I don't know." She looked around the Spanish tiled entryway, at the wrought iron stands, the vases and flowers—at everything she was leaving. But she couldn't look at me.

What confused me was how calm she was, her dewy skin with shimmering, peachy cheeks and her eyes open wide and clear. She wasn't supposed to look so at ease, so beautiful, so hopeful. She should have looked disheveled and sweaty from huddling her bags, moving them quickly towards the door. "You're moving there," I said setting one bag of groceries down.

"Stay here as long as you need," she said. "I don't need to sell it right away."

I shake my head. I couldn't stay here, not without her.

She unlocked the door, opened it, kept it propped open with her foot so it wouldn't close prematurely. "Everyone's moving on, Eva. You're an adult now. You'll be fine. I'll visit, and you're in New York a lot."

"I'm not in New York a lot," I said. My mind went blank, I couldn't find my thoughts, I felt the shock settling in, like a freezing liquid making its way across my skin until I couldn't feel anything anymore. I kept my eyes focused on the luggage tag, trying to make out the address that was lightly scratched out.

She shrugged her shoulders as if she didn't believe me. "You're almost 21. I was a mother by your age."

"I'm almost twenty," I said quietly, correcting her. My car keys were still in my hand, but I didn't want to set them down, hearing them clang on the stone countertop, echoing through a now empty house.

She opened her purse and looked for something, oblivious to what was happening. Why did she never know the simplest things? That I wouldn't be fine without her. Or why did it not click that she was the only family I had left or that I wanted her to know me, really know me—know a piece of information that no one else did. Like that I put marshmallows in my coffee on Sunday mornings while reading the Parade Section of the *Times*. Or why didn't she intuitively know that being able to share a home with her was the only bit of stability I had, that being able to walk in a room with framed photos and stacks of art, travel magazines and memoirs on the coffee table gave me a feeling of normalcy. Home with her was a place to think of when I was away on location where nothing was worn-in, lived-in or familiar.

"Richard's still around," she said, after she found the lipstick, she was looking for.

"It's obviously not the same," I said, and I hated that my voice cracked.

She looked at me, no expression, not knowing or having anything to say.

Someone buzzed at the gate and she pressed the button to let them in. "I'll call you when I land at Kennedy."

A driver in a dark suit walked up the steps. "All these go," she said, and he took the bags three at a time.

As simple as if she were going to drop off dry cleaning or pick up coffee beans from the local store, she adjusted her purse and looked around. Then she glanced over her shoulder and I thought I saw her lips quiver. "I have to go," she said, her voice soft and there was no sound when she shut the door.

I leaned against the cold stone of the kitchen counter and let myself slide down until I hit the floor. I pulled my knees to my chest and hugged them tight the way I learned to do as a child when no one was around to soothe me when I was afraid or woke from a bad dream. I couldn't get up, the same question repeating in my head again and again. Why was it so easy for her to go, to leave me? There was no struggle, no moment of pause. I kept listening for her keys or the lock to click open or a car door slam, or footsteps coming up the front steps. But there was only quiet, and then the drip of water from the faucet that was never fixed becoming deafening against the silence.

CHAPTER
EIGHT

Two airport greeters help unload our bags at Burbank Airport. Traffic buzzes by, and there's an array of horns, whistles. I keep my head low, and I tuck my hair up into my hat. Isabelle does the talking and arranging, shows our tickets and gives instructions. Lily shuts the trunk and adjusts my collar. I kiss her on the cheek and tell her to come visit. Her soft rose scent she's worn for twenty years drifts around me. I breathe in, the smell always centers me, it means she is close enough to touch, to reassure. Isabelle kisses her on both cheeks and doesn't know what to say.

We walk through the airport and I'm glad Isabelle booked the last flights. Just a few people are scattered through the terminal and the shops are closed. I feel okay, and not as nervous as I thought I'd be. There's no panic and I don't feel eyes on me that aren't there.

Isabelle stays close and holds her breath when she thinks someone's looking too long or if they hold up a phone, tilted in our direction. Once in a while she glances over at me and gives a small smile, a tiny nod she doesn't think I notice. If I didn't know better I'd say she's proud to be walking next to me. How long has it been this way? I'd always been the one who stole side-glances at her, noticed people staring at her, jealous or appraising eyes, smelled her perfume when she bumped me or reached over me—a breeze of wisterias.

The attendants lead us through a side door to the VIP Lounge. Isabelle's flight leaves almost an hour after mine. She tucks a loose piece of my hair under my hat and then grabs a magazine from her bag and ushers us to corner, dimly-lit seats in the back. I know she doesn't want a scene as much as I don't.

When a group of men sit down near us, I don't turn but I'm sure they're wearing business suits. They're talking about the Sonics beating the Lakers. Isabelle whispers she wished I'd taken Richard's offer to fly private.

"I told you," I say. "I don't want to start out that way, sitting on a plane all alone because I was afraid to face the outside world." She shook her head for what seemed like the hundredth time since she came.

Flight 225 to Seattle/Tacoma is announced open for check-in. I keep waiting for Isabelle to turn and say, "How could you not have insisted I come?" or "Please don't go." All the things I wished I said to her all the years ago when she left for New York. Since Richard told her the plan, she had been nothing but disapproving, judgmental, even tried to get Dr. Rose to convince me not to go.

"Are you still okay about doing this?" Isabelle asks as she places the magazine back in her bag.

I nod. "You're welcome to visit while we're there. There's more than enough room." I look up as more people come in to the lounge.

"It's nice in New York right now. The Christmas lights will soon be up," she says, tucking her hair behind her ears.

For the last decade I've been waiting for her to tell me she was ready to move back to Los Angeles, expected her to come to me and explain that she'd just needed a hiatus, a change of pace, or better theatres. But as I look at her now, her eyes are hopeful with anticipation, the same way they were when she moved all those years ago. Her clothes are darker and are more tailored. I know she loves it there, maybe even tells people she's from there, no trace of twenty years in California left in her.

People with children start to line up to board and I wish I'd left Isabelle a letter for her to find in her bag or jacket pocket, or sent an email that would be waiting in her inbox when she landed. To say thank you for staying longer than I ever thought she would, for leaving up the picture of Sam when he was fifteen and just won a local surf competition, a big smile, gangly limbs, a pale blue swim shorts stuck to his thighs. And I especially wanted to thank her for trying to act and create a normal household of three women. She scheduled my colorist and manicurist to come to the house after she noticed I started getting dressed in the mornings. She reserved a tennis court every Wednesday and Friday morning instead of telling me it was unhealthy to stay inside for days. When I had set backs, she allowed me to lie in bed some afternoons when the sadness felt paralyzing. And I appreciated her for preparing a late lunch of lobster from the fish market while telling me Planet Blue had gotten in a new shipment of sweaters, instead of suggesting I'd been in my room, curtain drawn, long enough. For being everything, she was and wasn't.

All the good and bad from our years together forced me to become who I am, nudged me to a level of success I never dreamed of in the past. The times I felt starved for love, affection, acceptance caused me to long to be other people, to easily attach to other identities, to wonder and inhabit different lives other than my own. I could play women with loud, extended families around rectangular dinner tables with flowery place settings, who met in cabins in the Tetones or Smokey Mountains at Thanksgiving just as the first snow fell. It all helped train me to be able to become someone else's daughter, drawn to roles where the mother was earthy and grounded, wore turtlenecks in the winter and flowing, Indian tunics in the summer, had graying temples and created a home that smelled of batter and lemons. It caused me to gravitate to a profession, to films, to worlds where everything was resolved at the end, where you knew what was coming the next day, that if you just waited long enough, the antagonist would self-destruct and that the person you loved would always come back.

Our handler returns and tells us that I will board as soon as everyone is on the plane. "You ready for this?" Isabelle's hand touches my arm, pulling me from my thoughts.

I don't know if I can get on this plane. "I don't think I can do it," I whisper.

"You're going to be good," she says, cutting me off, taking my hand, maybe afraid for me to finish what I was going to say. "You've been through the worst of it." She looks down, unsure.

Have I? Does she promise? I don't know how to leave her or leave things between us. She is one of those people I feel better being angry at, or standing across from shouting my disgust, than leaving.

"You should head over soon," she says, not letting go of my hand.

She isn't the only one who knows about leaving. Now, I know too. I'm learning about forcing myself out the door, packing a bag that you don't even remember what is inside. All for what? To save or find what is left of the strongest part of yourself?

I watch Isabelle zip up my carry-on, after trying to figure out if I have my ticket. They announce the main cabin is boarding, I notice her hands shake a little and I all of a sudden understand why she left all those years ago. She was only forty and was doing what she should have done long before I was born, or before my father left her. She built a life outside of what everyone else wanted from her or needed or expected.

I stand, not sure if I can, hold on to her tight and pick up my bag. "Thank you," I say. "For staying with me." It's all I can choke out.

"Call when you land." She hugs me, she feels thinner. She lets go and I stumble forward. I'm still holding on.

I nod. "I love you," I say. Both of us look at each other in surprise. How many times have I said that to her or her to me. Not enough.

Her eyes turn a darker brown and moisten. She squeezes my hand and then walks away, looking down, her ruffled faux mink coat engulfing her slight frame.

As she rounds the corner, she throws her head back and disappears.

And maybe that's enough and maybe it isn't. But if nothing else, it's a starting place.

Rain drops blur the airplane window and I reach up to wipe the moisture off. I stop, surprised at how normal my hand looks and feels. The deep purple nail polish a surprise after having nothing on for so long. I don't picture my wedding band there, don't feel the indents of the diamonds around my finger anymore. I look out, the plane's wheels just touched down, the Alaska Airlines terminal getting closer. A floodlight guides our way, through a light Seattle fog. I breathe in, the dull ache in my stomach that's been there since I can remember has disappeared. As if somewhere between Los Angeles and Seattle, the altitude change, the miles dissolved the pressure, the emotion that I've carried there.

Everyone around me stands up before the fasten seat belt sign blinks off. In a hurry, turning on cell phones, edging into the aisle. I don't make eye contact with anyone and run my hand across the empty seat next to me. No one could tell me why there was a vacant first-class seat next to me on an oversold flight. When I'd questioned the flight attendant she'd looked away, and handed me another flute of champagne and extra peanuts. My instinct is Richard bought the seat so I could fly without worrying about small talk.

The older couple across the aisle takes one last glance my way and reach for their carry-ons slowly, pretending to focus on something just beyond me. I nod at them, my way of thanking them for being so careful the entire flight, not gawking or striking up conversation, or taking out their phones. I stand but don't even bother looking in the overhead. There is nothing of mine there. I didn't bring any trinkets—books or jewelry or pictures that remind me of where I'd come from or who I've been.

The airport's damp and cold fluorescent lights are flickering as I walk quickly through the terminal, following closely behind the Greeter—but not too fast. I stare at the beams that run along the ceilings, and then on the ground, but never straight ahead.

A camera flash goes off and I turn my face—a reflex that seems old, forgotten. I'm afraid to see if it's for the couple posing with red carnations or if the dark lens is lingering on me. Maybe I'm paranoid? The baggage claim sign is getting closer and I finally turn around as I step on the escalator. But Dr. Rose's words force me to be kinder to myself. She'd said, "Some paranoia is normal in your line of work. Especially after everything you've been through."

I round the corner; Grace is standing next to the baggage carousel wearing jeans and an off the shoulder cowl neck ivory sweater that I instantly want to borrow. It looks Seattle, probably feels like Seattle—oversized but homey. She doesn't see me for a long time and then lifts her chin and gives a small smile. Despite everything, the year of not really talking, her obvious anger at me, I still love her. She's the only hint of left of Sam. The good parts.

Grace takes my luggage from the greeter and says the car's just right there. I thank her for being so cautious, parking close and waiting for me. We both let out sighs when we walk outside, no cameras and no one there to notice us or me. An officer nods as we approach her Land Cruiser. He takes the bags from Grace's hands and sets them in the back of her car. He doesn't look too long at me; he's staring at Grace.

There's no traffic, just occasional headlights glowing orange in the rearview mirror. My hand is on the armrest as Grace reaches for her glasses and her fingers brush mine. She jerks her hand and apologizes. Am I fragile to her? Does she still think of me, buried in blankets in a bed permanently unmade, refusing to turn when she'd come to say goodbye after the funeral, a smear of mascara blackened tears and tan make-up on my pillows?

"We'll just make it," she says as she pulls out of the airport. "The last ferry's at ten."

I don't know what to say yet, can't remember the name of the town where the ferry is, what the Northwest smells like or the way there. So, I turn on the radio and try to remember the route to the boat terminal, suddenly feeling like I need to, just in case this is the beginning of a trip I'll make again and again.

What it is that's so fascinatingly uncomfortable about sitting with someone you know in silence? Especially when it's someone you have a history with, someone you should have plenty to talk about, a long list of memories to recall—but nothing surfaces, there's no words left to configure.

Grace grips the steering wheel, it's been forty-nine minutes of quiet since we left the airport, passing trees and hills along the I-5. If you can sit in silence, does it mean you know each other better? Does the silence between us mean that we are old, comfortable friends at peace with quiet? Or does it mean we're no longer linked, the minutes ticking away, just reminders that time apart untethered the bond. I start to feel the tension return to my stomach, so I think about what Dr. Rose said, about the healing process. That it's about reconnecting to the world and re-establishing relationships. "It takes time," she'd said. "It takes sitting with the uncomfortable, the unknown. Letting it unfold."

Once in a while, Grace points out signs along the highway, turn-offs promising long roads to Bellingham, Bellevue, Blaine and Aberdeen. When she says the names, they have a sweet, folk rhythm.

I watch as she scrolls through her playlists on the center counsel touch screen and stops on a M83 album.

We exit Highway 20 west towards Mount Vernon, and I hear the first few chords of the French Electronic music.

"Anacortes," I repeat the town's name and then remember. The city where the ferries come and go, Sam used to say when we were kids. "Do you already have the tickets?" I ask her.

She shakes her head. "We'll get them at the terminal."

I almost remind her that I haven't been here in over twenty years, but decide not to bring it up. She knows. I look around; I'm surprised that despite the dark, I can see how it's changed. The usual additions: 7-11, liquor stores with pink neon signs, strip malls with a few parking lot lamps flickering amber, houses battered by negligence and constant dense sea air off the Sound are all here. As we twist down the road, trees cluster from the pavement to the water and then, an outline of the ferry, with floodlights running the length of the bough and fluorescent bulbs shines through large windows. Grace pays and pulls into the boarding lane, behind a black truck.

"Maybe we should stay with the car," she says.

She's worried about someone recognizing me. "It's okay," I say. The people around us are wearing earth-tone ski hats and puffy jackets, carrying books, duffel bags and sleeping children. They don't seem the kind that would notice, look or care. But we stay put anyway.

I start to worry that I've forgotten the keys to the house, or Richard's directions to the cottage, or my black thermal, or my favorite tea. Or are they nerves just because it's so awkward between Grace and me—why do I suddenly feel like I'm traveling with a stranger?

The ferry cuts a zigzag course between islands covered with trees atop black water. From a plane they look like navy clouds. I breathe in the fumes from the ferry and algae and charred pines. Grace is asleep already, or pretending, her head back, her glasses on a cord around her neck, a jacket tucked up to her chin.

A car door opens, and I watch as a man helps a pregnant woman out, puts a jacket around her shoulders and I can't help but remember —what it felt like to be her: morning sickness, night sickness, aching joints and fuller breasts. And then, what I felt like to not be anymore. Laying in a hospital room, not pregnant. For two days I was Alice Jones. The alias was typed on my hospital wristband, on the top of my medical charts and then again on my release papers. I even signed the name, inventing a new signature, pretended I looked like an Alice Jones—imagined she was petite with jet black hair, large lilac-colored eyes, and a nose too small for her face. Lying in that private room on a private floor, I kept glancing over at Lily, asking her if anyone knew. She'd shake her head, take my hand and say, your anonymity was protected, guaranteed here. She'd remind me again, we did all the right things, took all the right precautions—she drove instead of calling an ambulance, we came through the surgeon's entrance. I was in the last room at the end of a hall and there was no record of Eva Douglas. Only an alias, who has lost a child.

The ferry horn sounds twice, pulling me away from my thoughts—we're almost there. I tell myself it's over, it's a memory now. I remind myself what Dr. Rose always said, to not Band-aide the experience. When there's a trigger, something reminds you of the bad experience, you lean into it and ground yourself in the here and now. So, I lock eyes with the man in the car next to us and we stare. I have no hat, no glasses; it's just me, my hair down, wavier from the damp wind. He smiles, he's older. The lines on his face deepen when he grins and then he looks away. Maybe he's a fisherman, or someone who cuts lumber, or he owns vineyards. His car is ashy with oxidation from the sea air.

"How long did I sleep?" Grace says opening her eyes. She shifts in the driver's seat, and then looks at the cars parked around us, behind us, lets out a deep breath when she sees the cove ahead.

"Almost an hour," I say.

She turns down the heat, leans forward to gauge by the landmarks where we are. "It shouldn't be too much longer," she says. "Want a hot chocolate or something? I need to pee."

I shake my head as she gets out of the car. Ahead, patchy dots of apricot lights brighten an isthmus with clouds drawn overhead like stretched cotton.

"Friday Harbor," I say, even though there's no one here to listen or respond.

♮

What I notice first is the smell. Bath salts and baked maple and dry, Christmas tree pines browning just after the New Year.

Its early morning and everything here changes when it's overcast. The marine layer brings softer scents, clearer colors. I'm standing on the freshly painted deck, built on stilts buried between rocks, disappearing in the shallow water. I hear music inside and water running. Grace must be doing dishes, or starting the dishwasher or washing machine; neither one of us can sleep. For the last week we've been wandering around the house, opening drawers, cupboards, rearranging ceramic plates, washing and folding sheets and duvets that already smelled new. Grace obsessed with getting everything clean.

"It feels like rain," Grace says, standing at the patio door, holding a mug.

I have a coffee in my hand, a few drops on my sleeves. There's a light breeze off the water, and I'm glad we're in a small cove, the curve of the land shielding us heavy during winds.

"Have you talked to your mom yet?" she asks.

"We've been playing phone tag," I say. "But we've texted." I don't tell her I haven't been on the phone at all, I've been avoiding it. I've spent all my time looking through rooms and closets, arranging the new clothes I'd bought on someone else's hangers. I've sat in the large indigo velvet couch with sheltering arms, reading, losing myself in books. I've taken long runs, following the water's edge, the rhythm of my pounding feet, the sweat turning cold quickly with the damp air cleansing my system.

We don't talk for a while, and suddenly it's almost more than I can stand, tabulating the last few days of only speaking occasional words about trivial things, what channel we wanted to watch on T.V., or what show on Netflix. Going to bed earlier and earlier and waking before the sunrise. A lot of "I don't cares" or "Whatever you want to do today."

"Do you want to go into town today?" I say and take a sip of coffee. The small little town, the few blocks of Main Street, is such a mystery to me. Intrigue. It feels like a fresh start, so much to explore, with new shops, cozy sweaters engulfing mannequins, stain glass lamps and glossy stationary in the windows, new things, new people. The thought gives me the courage to do what Dr. Rose suggested: re-enter the world, the mundane, the routine.

She doesn't answer and sits in the chair across from me and sets one of her textbooks in her lap. "Why didn't you tell me you were pregnant," she says finally. Her fingers leaf through the pages mindlessly.

The mug starts to slip through my hand, the ceramic suddenly feeling slimy. I grab it with the other hand and take a deep breath. My first instinct is to change the subject, or get up. The word pregnant, the two-syllable noun that brings happiness, hope, anticipation to so many people but it's a trigger word for me. It brings shame, guilt, anger, grief. I look down, count to ten. Dr. Rose's voice in my head, the way her tone softens and strengthens as she says *"Don't be afraid of what hurts. Lean in."*

I close my eyes, think about when I found out I was pregnant, and later sitting at the kitchen table alone. Sam and I had a huge fight, he hadn't been home in two days. I stared out at the ocean in front of our beautiful new house for hours, the positive test on top of the box on the counter. I wondered if this is what it felt like to have everything you're supposed to have and want—a custom beach front home, a successful career, a good-looking husband, a baby on the way. Only I wasn't feeling the happiness that all of it promised. Everything I built felt staged, for show, the foundation and structure assembled on quicksand and it was just minutes away from buckling and being swallowed.

"Is this why we haven't really talked this last year," I ask.

She nods. "I think partly," she says. "There is so much I feel like I didn't know. But, I need to know, now, to understand." She clears her throat because her voice is shaky and I know how hard this is for her. For both of us.

"I didn't tell anyone, even your brother. I wasn't sure what I was going to do," I say. I close my eyes and shake my head hearing the shame in my voice. "You know how your brother felt. The deal. He didn't want kids. Always said, absolutely no kids."

"You should have told him, or me, regardless. Let me be there for you." She crosses her legs; her blue nail polish looks stark against her pale toes. "I thought we were closer than that. I thought we all were." I hear the anger in her voice, the disappointment.

"I know I let you down," I say. "I'm sorry." I couldn't tell anyone. My decision had to be so well thought out. I needed time to get stronger, so when I did tell Sam, it wouldn't have mattered what he said, or if he left. My choice to have the baby had to be resistant to threats and pleas. I needed time to learn about laying a solid foundation under my feet. Finding my own space. I needed to excavate anything detrimental to growth: tree roots, diseased weeds that would rob the soil beneath of essential nutrients needed to sustain the weight of what I had to build.

"You should have told him," she says again, ignoring my apology.

"You think that would have made a difference? He would have left anyway or sooner." I feel myself starting to get angry, hate the defensiveness in my tone.

Her whole body is tense and she shuts the textbook.

"This is going nowhere," Grace says.

"You brought it up," I say. I'm grateful for the anger I feel. It's easier. It insulates the pain underneath.

"You're right," she says looking at me dead on. "And I shouldn't have."

She stands and I know I have to say something, to push through this wall. I feel our six-year age difference for the first time in a long time. She doesn't understand. I feel the responsibility that comes with being slightly older.

"It was over between your brother and me, Gracie. You know that."

She turns quickly, as if her childhood nickname jarred her, pulled her from whatever she was thinking, her anger. She slowly sits back down, as if unsure of what to do next. "I don't believe that," she says sadly. "He would have come around." Her tone is now hopeful, unsure, trying her best to convince herself and me.

He wouldn't have come around and neither would I. The second I found out I was pregnant; I felt a confidence and clarity I hadn't really known. Like duct tape ripped from my eyes with no warning, or count down. Even though I couldn't protect myself, extradite myself from my situation, my unhappiness, I knew I could do it for my child. If he didn't want us, I knew I wouldn't fight him, beg him to stay.

Looking at her, huddled into the rusty red patio pillows, her feet tucked under her, childlike, I recognize in her now what I must have looked like, sounded like before all this happened. I, too, was some-one who had been blinded by childhood attachment, walled in by the loyalty that develops between children. The strong bond that's formed in youth's vulnerability and in young heartbreak. It was a union that kept us afloat in the times it felt like it was just the three if us, clinging to each other in a life raft, bobbing out at sea. We were too young to realize dysfunction was forming, growing like algae, its barnacles attaching to the bottom of our raft, inadvertently creating a drag. We all suffered a lack of maneuverability and a slow, silent corrosion, poked with holes and tiny tears that would expand in time. And then eventually, the cold whirling water would seep in, sinking the only thing that kept us together.

"You can't honestly believe that a baby would have saved us?" I ask quietly, instantly regretting the question. Maybe I was being too hard, pushing her to get to a place she wasn't ready to go. The grief I felt for my baby was different than what I felt for Sam. One was a dull, whispering ache, a voice calling for me in a mirrored labyrinth. The other, an acute pain—a panicky loss. The past wiped clean.

"I do," she says, not looking at me.

"You blame me." I've been so afraid of this conversation for so long.

"It isn't about blaming someone, Eva."

She still can't look at me and it's obvious that's what has been keeping us apart—we both blamed me without meaning to, and somewhere in her grief, she chose to put it all on me. The confusion, the torment, all of the things she wasn't ready to feel and face, she chose to idealize. This way she could hold Sam in a certain light, statuesque and atop a glossed marble pedestal. She could retain her long-haired, noble, protective brother who mostly did the right thing, eventually, even if it was too late. I start to say something, to question her further, but stop. Dr. Rose's words coming to mind again. *"Just because you're ready to start the journey on your road to healing doesn't mean anyone else is. You need to respect that. Wait for them to join you."*

"He was afraid," Grace continues. She pushes her bangs away from her eyes but they immediately fall forward. "That's why he didn't want a kid. Because of our childhood and he raising me when he was just a kid himself."

I see for the first time that as much as I clung to Sam in the lifeboat, she hung on tighter. She was always younger, smaller, her adoration of him palpable.

"I know," is all I can say. It would feel cruel to say anything else. The wind is picking up and two kayakers paddle by. One lifts his yellow oar in greeting. Grace and I both automatically wave back.

She plays with the corner of the textbook where the edge is caving in. It's not the right time to force anything else. Tell her that her brother wasn't perfect, point out that it was always his way, that everyone who loved him clung to the little he would give, anxiously awaiting the moments he would let his guard down, reveal himself. Those moments could hold you over months, even years.

"I can't talk about this anymore," she says.

"I understand," I say. I was there, too, maybe still am, one foot in, one foot out.

She gets up, tosses her coffee in a nearby planter and shuts her eyes tightly, shakes her head as if she's trying to erase a visual, something she's not ready to see or remember. Is she picturing what I have countless times before? Does she see Sam right before his accident, the moment before impact, his head down, his scuffed boots and jeans hugging the bike, eyes clear, unafraid, wind caught in the back of his jacket, all sound stopping.

"I'm gonna start breakfast," Grace says, closing her sweatshirt around her. "Then I got to get back to my thesis."

I reach out my hand as she walks by; she takes it but looks straight ahead. With her touch, for a second everything feels like it used to, our connection starting as two young girls, oblivious in that life raft.

She drops my hand, letting go and walks inside.

CHAPTER
TEN

Chapstick and driving. The things that always made me feel closest to Isabelle.

Putting on my lip balm now, slowing the car down on the long stretch into town, deer crossings signs and wheat-colored fields of alpacas all around me, I think of her. Isabelle. The hours we spent in the car when I was a child, her smearing Chapstick every half hour over her plump lips, watching the road, stressing the importance of skin hydration when sitting in front of air-conditioning or heat. Running her hands over her mouth, then mine, saying there is nothing worse than allowing chapped lips. How they aged you. Then she'd grow quiet and turn up the radio. It never mattered if it was the Stones or Willie Nelson—we would sing, without tension, no shame. During her favorite parts the songs, I'd glance over at her; we'd get louder, tilt our heads back, with our hair always falling the same length down our backs. She'd look at me quickly, or sometimes longer. The road would blur, and in those moments, I felt like Isabelle was my mother.

At the fire station on the edge of town, I look for a parking space. I like leaving the car a ways from the grocery store, loving the walk, looking at the glass trinkets in the small shop windows, seeing my reflection, sometimes not recognizing myself. Someone with wavier hair, simpler clothes. Checkered flannel shirts, baggier jeans, and boots with thick tread.

I step out of the car and don't know how two and a half months has passed here already. The holidays came and went so quietly. So much time spent outside, clothes smelling permanently of saltwater and rosemary. With each morning that passed, I saw myself changing every time I looked in the bathroom mirror. I saw somebody softer, hair tousled and longer, rested eyes, lighter, clearer skin, natural flushed cheeks—wondering if I might be somebody more like me or who I would have become if I'd chosen a different path.

I button my coat as I make my way towards Friday Harbor Grocery. I think about Grace, how she'd smirked as I was leaving this morning, saying, "Third trip into town in four days, Eva." I'd replied that we need almond milk and more protein powder even though we probably didn't. I couldn't explain to her that I looked forward to the walk on Main Street, the view of the ocean, the ferry dock busy with men yelling in orange waders and yellow shiny parkas, the smell of fried fish cooking for lunchtime. People smiled at me, but never spoke. Grace would laugh or think I needed to be recognized, watched, maybe she was right or wasn't. There's a chance she wouldn't believe me when I said there is an accomplishment in something so easy as dragging myself out the door. Maybe I'm discovering a different life, as somebody else, or weaving together the old me and the new. Understanding how I'm different now, on different terms, still not a hundred percent sure of what to do with the past, where to place it.

A woman pushes a stroller on the other side of the street; stopping to look at something in a window and a car passes and honks. A pregnant cashier glances up as I walk in the store and grab a basket. She smiles and so do I. The market looks pulled out of the past. Small pastel kites and multi-colored wind sockets hang from the ceiling and sway in unison every time the doors slide open and closed. I chose a few things, along with postcard with a picture of the island at night. I look up from the cards and make eye contact with a man who smiles and nods. I say hello, suddenly worried I don't blend in even though I'm dressed as I am, an islander.

In the checkout line, I wait behind a woman with a small child who stares at me from behind her mother's leg. I listen to the cashier talk about her husband as she punches in numbers. She smiles, her eyes larger when she says his name, how they had fun at the fire station BBQ this past weekend, how this is a slow time for firemen, not much action on the island with the damp winter air from the Sound. Neither of them looks at me and I make eye contact with the child and smile. I take my things out of the basket and briefly envy the woman on the other side of the register, the picture she paints of normalcy so alluring: backyard parties, making enchiladas from scratch, blowing up balloons until your cheeks hurt.

"How're you?" the cashier says as she picks up the milk, the sleeves of her sweater rolled up revealing a flesh-colored scripture tattoo on her forearm I can't make out.

"Good," I say and I know I sound awkward or nervous. It's the first time she's addressed me; I've passed her in the coffee shop and again in the one room museum by the water's edge.

She runs my items over the scanner, takes a long time punching in numbers on the register, awkwardly, as if she's learning but doesn't want anyone to know. I put my credit card on the counter.

"I've been seeing you around," she says. "On vacation?"

She's younger than I thought. Her blonde hair is pulled up in a messy top knot, and gold hoops swing back and forth when moves. There's the beginning of crow's-feet when she smiles. I guess she's around my age.

—"I rented a place for a while," I say. I look around and the store is empty.

"Eva, right?" she asks putting things into my reusable bags. She says my name with ease, like an old friend and it startles me. But I'm distracted by how she's piling things in, putting bananas and milk on top of the bread and Asian pears. She's oblivious and I can't help but smile.

She stops and looks up because I haven't answered.

"Yes," I say. "Eva." I hear my voice shake. She's heard about me and I know I must have been ignorant, thinking no one has noticed me here or cared. Grace and I made a pact not to sign online while we were here. Everyone else in my life pretended there was no news. After Russ released my statement, declined interviews, after the press camped out at the bungalow where I had been staying before the premiere, went away, I told myself it was over. My house in Malibu was registered in a trust, and my neighbors were discreet. But I wonder, if I went online, Googled my name, would I find a picture of me coming out of the coffee shop posted on Twitter, hood pulled over my head, with a caption, "Found."

As I look at the cashier, I can't help but wonder, if she's read everything, if she knows about my life—if she's read Wikipedia, making my life appear better and worse than it is.

She shifts her weight, uncomfortable too—suddenly nervous as if she senses she's upset me. "Your name is on the credit card."

We look at each other and smile. She reaches over and puts her hand on mine and squeezes.

As she bags the rest of the things, I can't help but be paranoid. Are people talking, whispering, do they know what house we're in? All this time, I was hoping for something that can never happen— that I can fit in, blend, eventually become someone other than a visitor or someone from 'out of town.' I glance at the tabloids at the edge of the register. I'm not on there, never have been on the front cover. Thankfully not an actress whom the world and long tele-photo lenses and sweaty men in beat up Corolla's stalk. I've never had a high-profile love affair, been out late at clubs or frequented Sunset Tower. Russ said my premiere incident died on the vine after a week and a half when the next scandal came along. At the most, he said, it was way down the page on Daily Mail, a small blurb on page eight of *Us Weekly*.

"I'm Kristin," she says. "People call me Kris, actually."

There was something about her, a voice, sweet and young, but her gestures and expressions older. I can wish for that she doesn't recognize me from anything and knows nothing about me. And that taking the time to look at a customer's name on a credit card is one of the intimacies of a small town.

There's silence and I wait for her to ask about a movie or if Ryan Gosling is as gentlemanly as he seems or if Shia Le Bouf is short in person. She doesn't.

"You up here alone?" she asks.

I shake my head. "With a friend." Why didn't I tell her the truth? There's no need to be paranoid, Hollywood is not up here. No movie stars here, chum in the water for a photographers to descend upon. I haven't noticed taking a picture with a phone or pretending to text but actually recording. Russ assured the press doesn't know where I am and doesn't care. It's nothing like L.A., when you walk certain streets holding your head up, like looking in the mirror, alert, eyes scanning, taking in everything.

I fumble with my wallet and try to put it back in my purse. She's finished bagging and I'm lingering.

"How do you like the island?" she asks and hands me my credit card back.

"I like it a lot. It's colder than I thought."

The door chimes as three men walk in, paint splattered on their hands and sweatshirts, hats pulled down or on backwards. I look away. One of them whistles and Kris calls out, saying hello and rolls her eyes. "Good 'ol local boys. Went to high school with my husband."

"Must be nice to know people your whole life," I say. I missed that, the group of friends going through school together, going to college, coming home for the holidays to the local bar. I was auditioning, flying back and forth, sitting in long cold halls on folding chairs waiting to be called inside by a casting director who barely makes eye contact.

"Has it perks, I guess," she says. "And pitfalls." She puts a hand on her stomach and with the other slides a receipt over to me to sign. She has a baggy sweater on, but when she turns to the side she looks about five or six months pregnant.

"You're going to really like it up here. No matter how long you stay," she says.

I put the pen down, and switch my purse to the other shoulder. Her friendliness and sincerity catch me off guard.

She gets my bags together. "These islands up here have a way of making everything simpler, easier. Can't really explain." "I'm beginning to realize," I say.

"You might stay awhile, then," she says.

I nod and take the bags from her.

"If you or your friend need anything, recommendations on where to get a drink, hike, or someone to show you around," she says. "Let me know. I've lived here a long time."

The phone rings and I adjust the bags so I can carry them all. As she talks, her voice drops to a whisper. I wave and mouth goodbye. She smiles and covers the phone. "I'll be here the next couple weeks. Helping my in-laws run this place. The manager quit unexpectedly." She reaches out her hand and then pulls it away awkwardly. "So, don't be a stranger."

The doors slide open, my cue to go. I look back, she has the phone cradled against her shoulder, and she's nodding, rubbing circles around her stomach.

I walk slowly back to the car feeling relieved. Remembering what it feels like to be in the world, to run errands, to have a connection with someone in a random place. It feels like it's been years since I stopped to talk to someone or met someone who was interested in me—who wasn't on a film set or a friend of Sam's. I think about how it was before marrying him or getting together in Spain, when it was just me. Those years filled with working odd jobs, waitressing, being a fit-model, driving across town for auditions in furniture-less, cold buildings with barren hallways. I'd fly back and forth from L.A. to N.Y., following the next job, meeting people on planes and airports and audition rooms. Always positive and negative feedback came from a casting director, as well as small parts, with more endless auditions and callbacks—constantly being told who I was and wasn't: too young, too old, too tall, too serious, too happy, too sad. I felt always on the edge of a breakthrough, always on the verge of quitting. And then things changed one afternoon when I got the call about a part in a David Lynch movie. The write-up in the *New York Times* stated I was a breakthrough actress with depth beyond my years. Shortly after, Richard's voice hummed over the phone, serious and quiet, saying, "This is it, kid. Don't look back."

I set the groceries in the back of the car, grateful that this woman, a stranger in a store, if only for fifteen minutes, gave me a glimpse of anonymity. A porthole into how I was before everything changed— before my world expanded and then contracted with loss.

CHAPTER
ELEVEN

The last time Sam and I made love—
I think about that as I drive back from town, the air and the steering wheel chilling from the temperature drop of the offshore approaching storm. I try and tell myself it wasn't real because I never wanted to believe I actually could pinpoint the last time I touched him. Those last weeks before he died were all just a blur and blended together-touch, glance, words, yelling, and tears, packing and unpacking.

I merge left, see the turn to the house and can still feel how his ribs fit under my breasts, how even though I was so mad at him, felt belittled from our fight an hour before, I listened, responded as he told me what to do in a soft, husky voice. His body rigid, grip tight under my back, my hair tangled in his hand. The anger always excited him. He'd whispered, please don't move, and then inhaled deeply. Neither one of us really able to look at each other-my face turned and his buried in my neck. The room so dark, windows open, smells of sea air dampness, mustard, sweat and mushy sand. Just as it ended, I glanced at the door, something reflective caught my eye—a silver parka, his clothes in a pile and a bag. The sheets cold, gray and indented in the morning after he was gone.

I grip the wheel and recall the exact night, date, and hour. The intimacy in my memory, suddenly no longer idealized, suddenly so imperfect, a last ditch at communication we were never good at. But his touch, firm and deep. At times, I still feel it on my skin.

I slow the car and turn into the long-paved road, step on the brakes because I see a black Mercedes with blacked out tinted windows. The car so out of place among drooping trees and dirt roads. I'm yards from my circle driveway, but I ease off the gas pedal. The front door opens, and I see Grace's stubby pigtails before I see her face. She turns and smiles. I roll down the window anticipating she has something important to say.

"Richard's here," she says, her eyes widening and opens my door.

I walk up the front steps and then take them two at a time. I'm nervous, and clutch the grocery bags tight. I walk towards him. He's standing in the foyer, his hands in his pockets. I set the bags down and I'm not sure what to say so I walk into his arms, bury my face in his sweater, feel the itchy wool against my cheek. And when I let out a breath, I'm consumed with the scent of coffee and sesame. Grace's footsteps are getting more rapid in the kitchen, back and forth. I pull away from him and he smiles.

"Hi," he says.

I look up at him and seems the same, but different. He hasn't shaved in days and looks bulkier under the thick sweater. Grace sets down a tray on the coffee table.

"Let's sit," I say, taking off my scarf and walking into the living room. "I'm so happy to see you."

Grace pours coffee in ceramic blue mugs and I study Richard. The stubble on his face is showing traces of grey making his eyes appear a softer, paler blue. It's been eighteen years since we first met, ten since we became friends, occasional dinner and premiere companions. A little over a year since we've become close friends. And then in between all of it, there's been long periods of absence without speaking or seeing each other, losing touch especially after I got married—Sam never liking him or me spending time with him.

"Grace was saying that you two are thinking about getting a boat," Richard grins, even though he's trying not to smile. He crosses his legs as she hands him a mug.

"A small speed boat or Whaler," I say. "We have the dock and Grace is interested in getting up close to the marine life around here. "Especially the Orca pods."

"This is the spot to do it," he says.

Grace plops down next to me on the sofa.

"How's your thesis going?" he asks her.

She smiles, like she always does whenever someone asks her about her work. "Dragging. Never ending. But I've been getting a lot of writing done up here. Thinking about staying a little longer."

I look at her; see her hands tightly gripped around the mug. "That's good news," I say, smiling. "I didn't know you were thinking about staying."

"I just kinda decided," she says, shrugging.

Richard looks around the house, taking it all in. "This place is even better than the picture on the website," he says.

Grace sets down her mug, hard. "I'm surprised to see you. "I thought it was at least another month before you were done filming."

"We wrapped ahead of schedule," he says, looking at me. "Got ten episodes in the can."

"Congratulations," Grace says, crossing her legs. She looks back and forth between us.

"I was in San Francisco for a meeting and to scout for a potential location and thought I'd head over here." He looks at me and I don't hold the gaze. I haven't called him, my responses to his texts short and infrequent. I search his face to see if he's offended, hurt, if he's convinced I've been avoiding him and everyone from L.A., the business. I don't blame him for showing up unannounced. Like him, I don't trust that I would have discouraged his suggestion to come.

"How long can you stay?" I ask him, realizing that now that he's here, I don't want to think of him going. His presence already changes the atmosphere, lifts a tension. It feels lighter, safer, a deep voice floating through the house, the steadiness of his breath offsetting Grace's quick and nervous tone.

"A few days," he answers. "Haven't changed my return ticket yet. It was just kinda spur of the moment."

"Let me put your stuff in one of the guest rooms," Grace says, standing. She collects the empty mugs. "You can get settled."

"How about a walk before it gets dark," I say to them, my eyes on Richard.

"I want to finish up the pages I'm working on," Grace says, walking into the kitchen. "You guys go ahead."

"We can all go in the morning," I say, turning my head so I can see her. She's setting things in the dishwasher. Part of me determined to include her, part of me not sure if I'm ready to be alone with him, or hear what he has to say.

"You guys go," Grace calls firmly.

I turn back and face Richard. He nods, gives me a quick wink, like he has so many times before when I'm unsure.

I want to ask him why he really came, why he showed up, unannounced, like he was just island hopping or sailing by. Instead, we keep walking, the lights changing and the sun is about to disappear behind a wall of Evergreens.

"I could get used to this place," I say.

Out of the corner of my eye I see the corner of his mouth pull into a half smile.

When he looks up at the trees, I glance at him again, his wool coat buttoned to the top, his square-toed shoes clicking and the only sound as we pass houses built on stilts at the edge of the island. He's chilled, not used to the dampness, but won't complain. I don't know what to do or say, so I walk a little faster. I point out the broken-down mausoleum, pure white marble with dark veins running through it and the small graves within. A memorial to the first family that settled the island, I tell him, and smell wood burning and seasoned meat cooking on a grill. His silence makes me uncomfortable, like he's taking time to try and configure something poignant he needs to say. I fiddle with a quarter that I discovered in my jacket pocket. "Should we go a little farther?" I ask, looking down at his shoes.

He nods. "I'm going to have to buy some shoes in town. Only have dressier stuff with me."

"I can take you to town in the morning."

"Grace said dinner would be in an hour. We have time to walk, go further." He sniffs.

"She's turned into quite the chef," I say.

He gestures forward, we continue walking. "She seems happy to be around you. Very protective."

I shrug. I don't know. There's good days and uncomfortable ones. Ever since our conversation about my pregnancy and her brother when we first arrived, there's been no more deep talk, discovery, attempts at resolving any of the tension that drifts and idles beneath whatever it is we say. The strain has lessened as the days pass, eases with the more time we spend together doing fun, frivolous things. But at times it's like discovering a stranger you swear you've met before.

I walk a few steps ahead. The trees clear. An overgrown meadow leads to the water, with a grey battered lighthouse at the edge.

"I'm waiting for you to tell me that Russ wants to know what I want to do next," I say. "That I need to make a decision soon."

"That's not why I came," he says, his tone even, but I swear I can hear a hint of defensiveness or hurt.

"But he does, doesn't he?" I say, and pull my coat tighter around me. "I haven't been good at returning his texts or emails."

"That makes two of us," he says, slowing the pace.

"I'm really sorry," I say, softly.

"He's concerned. We both are. Silence is never a good sign."

I walk faster and his footsteps quicken, trying to keep pace with me. "I feel like if I talk to him, if I call him up, I'll have to make a decision. I'm not there yet."

"He's a friend, Eva. It doesn't have to be just business. He wants to know you are doing okay."

I look at him. His face is serious, lips pressed together. He believes everything he says, thinks about everything he says, it's always laced with thoughtfulness and some sort of wisdom you almost miss if you're not playing close enough attention.

"I can hear what he'll say," I tell him, smiling. "He'll say, '*You're an actor, Evie, that's what you know. It's what your gift is.*'"

Richard smiles. "And he'd be right."

I think of the girl I was when I first started out in the business. Hopeful, open. I remember watching and rewatching my first films. The girl on the screen believed in forgiveness, destiny and fate. I liked that girl, I envied her. She had the strength and insight to be different if she chose to be.

Richard puts a hand on the small of my back and we move to the side of the road as a car passes. After it disappears, he doesn't pull his hand away. I look up at him and see my breath in the air.

"I don't know the next step," I say. "Even if I wanted to go back, would anyone want me, take a chance on me after everything?"

The question hangs in the air as our footsteps move across the pavement.

"Russ knows all that," Richard says. "There's no hurry, no pressure."

We both know that isn't true. You have a shelf life in that town, a window of time to be forgiven. People forget easily, move on to the next.

I move closer to him and his hand presses tighter on my back. It feels unnatural and then way too natural.

"I'm confused," I say and his hand moves slightly towards my waist. "Torn." I feel his eyes looking me over.

A screen door shuts in one of the houses and when Richard pulls his arm away and it feels too sudden.

"Am I supposed to go back? To L.A., that life?" I ask, moving away, afraid now to meet his glance. I feel the anxiety forming, remembering the last couple of years, especially when things got really bad with Sam. How simple it was to keep boundaries in my work, that it became very difficult to separate from a role. The worse things got at home, in my life, the more I tried to completely disappear into the parts. And then eventually, the parts became part of me, long after the movies wrapped. It felt like I would spend months lost, in and out of a character, still wanting to respond to that other name, wanting to go home to that other life.

"You don't have to know that now," he answers.

"Don't I?" My tone feels harsh. Weren't people forgetting me, or remembering me only as they last saw me? Is that why he's here, to bring me back or remind me where I come from and my responsibilities? To remind me that there is another place and life away from these dripping trees, weathered houses on the water and the white and green island ferries?

"Let's head back," he says. "We can talk about this later, when you're ready."

I stop walking. "When will that be," I say.

"It'll come." He turns around, digs his hands deeper in his pocket.

Another car approaches, slowing and a woman stares as she passes. A few more cars drive by and we're forced to walk single file. "Island rush hour," I say, trying to lighten the mood between us, watching him in front of me and now, I'm the one trying to keep up with his pace. We don't talk until I can see the house, the white lights strewn along the dock gangway.

"You picked a good place," he says. "A good home."

I watch the back of his head as he talks, his hair is so much longer and hits just below the collar of his coat. I take a few quick steps until I'm beside him. He catches my glance and I smile. It's twilight and there are no streetlamps, and his eyes look navy blue. "I'm happy you like it here," I say, and I don't remind him what he already knows—I had nothing to do with this. He realized long before I did, this was the place I wanted to go.

sit up in bed and can't help but listen for Richard's familiar sounds. Especially how I remember him in the mornings—from all those years before when I stayed with him after Isabelle moved to New York, until I found my own place. I can still hear a sliding glass door being shut, the banging of tins against granite countertops, and the smell of the murky dark coffee. I grew to love the tiniest things, even the way he sliced a papaya. I would watch as he stood at the counter, the knife gliding, no sound, the veins in his right arm flexing. He'd stand close to me, the phone resting on his shoulder, nodding at something someone on the other end was saying. I smelled his cologne and spicy granola as the slices fell one by one into the bowl. I'd eat the pieces quickly off the top hoping he'd slice more. Sometimes he would, sometimes he was too distracted to notice.

I hear nothing now. It's still dark in my bedroom, not yet five, the red drapes obscuring the beginning of white morning light. It's so early, but I can't sleep. I don't know if it's the anticipation of someone new in the house or the confusion of what I felt on last night's walk with Richard. Or if all those years of waking up before everyone else to get to a film set or to a location or the gym were still engrained in me? It's an internal alarm clock that seems like it will always be there no matter what I chose to do. It's an automatic reminder, an anxiety that lingers and nudges me in my sleep. It told me to open my eyes before the alarm went off, especially when I was with Sam. I'd feel around in the dark for my workout tights, and Ugg boots, trying not to make a sound. He'd move every few minutes, letting out a frustrated breath, the comforter inching higher and higher until it eventually covered his head. His annoyance steadily worsened as the years went by, and then especially towards the end, when everything about me and my career became intolerable. He'd developed a brewing anger he could barely contain, a nervous energy eating at the baseline of my stomach when someone just saying hi to me on the street caused him to drop my hand. A man looking a little too long caused him to speed up, leaving me behind. A waitress in a restaurant wanting to talk a little bit longer made him want to get the check and leave, even if we weren't finished. My hair products and appointments for massages infuriated him, causing him to slam his hand on a counter, shout that I'm frivolous with money, that success had gone to my head. And the last year we were together, if I had a kissing or love scene, he wouldn't touch me for days, even weeks. In the mornings, I'd see blankets and pillows wadded up on the couch or an unmade bed in a spare bedroom. Every premiere I had to attend, he tried to back out of, making up an excuse. I held it all in until one day, when Isabelle called. I was driving down the 10 freeway and just hearing her voice caused me to cry, the exit signs becoming a blurry green through my tears. After I told her Sam wouldn't go to events with me anymore, she'd said, "The more successful you get, the worse it's going to get." When I started to disagree, she'd continued, her tone filled with annoyance. "He hasn't found what he loves, his passion. He ricochets. People like that feel like they are barely above water and cling to anything so they won't drown."

I arrange the pillows on the bed, reminding myself I don't have to be quiet now, limit my movements anymore. I put the large pillows behind the smaller ones and realize that what Sam first loved about me, became what he detested in me the most. He used to get excited about visiting me on set, there was pride as he watched from behind the cameras, off to the side, hidden between the light and boom stands. He felt protective walking down the street with me, a step or two ahead, my hand tightly in his. He liked walking into a premiere, being the guy in the dark suit that didn't say much, no expression, always in the corner of the photograph. Or waiting for me inside the theatre, seats saved like we were in high school seeing a sold-out movie, and I'd tuck my arm through his and rest my head on his shoulder and he'd whisper, "Proud of you, baby."

A door closes downstairs and I'm pulled from my thoughts. Is it Richard or Grace? One of them was already going out for a run or for the paper. When we got home last night, I forced myself to eat as I sat across from them. Not caring about the salmon and dill sauce in front of me or their polite banter, Grace's aggressiveness on topics such as the island tides or the real estate market not responding to the slight economic upturn. I could only focus on that walk he and I had, how there were moments I stopped noticing where we were, more concerned with my proximity to him; was I too close or too far? I thought of when he was ahead of me, how I could smell wafts of his cologne, it glided back, amber oil that felt like it settled on my skin. At some point I stopped pointing out trivial landmarks because I was too focused on how I came just to his shoulder. And when he'd put his arm on the small of my back, I had to fight gravity not to drift into the curve of his side. At certain moments I might have even stepped in too close to him. Once we were back home, I silently willed the phone not to ring, or that no one FaceTimed—and that it not be Isabelle or anybody who knew me. I worried they would hear or see something different in me, my facial expression, my voice and pick up on that I was changing or something was.

I get dressed, focusing on the fact that there are three people in the house now instead of two. We need more groceries, more of what Richard likes to eat—blueberries, mango, eggs, steak tomatoes and chunks of mozzarella. Maybe this will serve as my excuse to get out, go into town, gain some perspective before everyone meets around the breakfast table. I reach for my jeans as I walk to the closet. Without thinking, I put on a thermal, a newsboy hat, my hair in messy waves.

Downstairs, the curtains are still drawn and bluish light sprinkles the sofa in patches. It still smells like baked butternut squash. Just out the window the fog breaks in spots and I can see only parts of the dock. The house feels so different from yesterday. Smaller, cozier, as if a fireplace has just been turned off, and I'm still surrounded by remnants of subtle warmth and diminishing crackling light. I grab the car keys and see Richard's jacket hanging on the stand. I run my hand over the soft fabric as I walk by.

A bouquet of tiny bells jingles every time the coffee shop door opens. Cold air shoots in like an abrupt exhale of breath. I sit at a table in the corner, my back to the entrance, a section of the *Wall Street Journal* someone left lies sprawled in front of me. I rotate the warm mug in my hand, the coffee in front of me untouched. The waitress sets my bagel on top of the *Money and Investing* section and says, "Anything else, darlin'?" I look up, shake my head. Her eyes linger as if she's trying to decide something.

"Eva," someone says behind me.

I turn, shocked to hear my name.

"You're up early," Kris says looking at a menu in her hand. She glances over her shoulder at the counter, to catch someone's attention. "Only the fishermen are in here this early." She laughs.

She looks curvier since I saw her, more pregnant than I remember, her face rounder and features softer. Her hair tumbles down her back in blonde waves.

"Please sit," I say. "Join me."

I feel that connection still from the other night.

She sets her Louis Vuitton bag on the chair next to me, sees me eyeing it.

"Obnoxious, huh," she says. "A gift from my mother-in-law." She sits, slowly with her hand on her belly.

Before I can reply a man from the counter sets a cup of tea down carefully in front of her and gives her a warm look. "Hungry, kiddo?"

She shakes her head. "No, thanks, Cal. Ryan made something before he left this morning."

"Your husband's a fireman?" I make sure I remembered correctly, suddenly so interested in her, drawn to her warmth, and curious about what makes everyone so attentive to her.

She nods at me and thanks the manager.

"Did you grow up here?" I ask.

She takes a sip of tea, shakes her head.

I look down, not sure if I'm asking too much, too soon, unsure of manners or how to be an acquaintance. It's been so long.

"I was raised in New York," she says.

I take a bite of my bagel, trying to hide my surprise.

"You're surprised," Kris says.

"A little," I smile, embarrassed at my honesty.

"It's okay," she says, fiddling with the string of the teabag. "Everyone is."

"I've spent a lot of time in that city," I say.

"Doing films?" she asks.

Her tone is so nonchalant, so natural, I almost miss the question. Or maybe it *is* a question. An icebreaker, or the easiest way to let me know she's familiar with who I am.

"Yes," I say, finally. "Doing films, and press, etc . . ." I pick up my coffee because I don't know what else to do. "And I did a short run-on Broadway a few years back." What else does she know? Does she know all of it, or thinks she does? Does everyone in this place know, too? Do they all look at me and see ghostly images of me that played on *Access Hollywood* for a week.

"I had some trouble," I say, awkwardly. "Months ago, back in L.A." I feel like I have to spit it out, I don't know any other way.

"Don't say anything else," she says her voice firm. "It's none of my business."

But now I suddenly want to explain more and start from the beginning. She's the first stranger that's given me a chance. Most just look, wonder, come to their own conclusions, a look of sorrow or pity. I scoot to the edge of my chair, lean in, but stop. More people are starting to fill in. This isn't the place or time.

"I used to come up here when I was a kid," I say instead.

She stares at something behind me. "This place, the island, heals most things I've found."

Something in her expression changes and she plays with the diamond solitaire that hangs around her neck.

"I should probably head out," I say. "I still need to get breakfast for my crew." I reach for my bag. "I have a guest staying with us from out of town."

"Did I say too much?" She reaches inside her bag, searching for something, her voice choppy, nervous. "I'm so sorry."

"It's fine," I say. "I just have to get back." It wasn't entirely true, but I've had as much as I can take. I'm starting to feel everyone's eyes on me.

She hands me her card. "Here's my number," she says. "If you need anything. If you and your friends want an insider's tour of the Island . . . "

"Thank you," I say, taking the card. I smile and do my best to reassure her, I squeeze her hand when she extends it. I don't look at anyone on the way out, and cringe when the door chimes go off. I close my jacket around me and cross the street to the market.

I have no idea what time it is, how long I'd been because the town traffic is picking up and stores are opening. In the market, I wander through the aisles, pick up things that feel like winter and Richard—coconut almond granola, dark apples, playing cards, breakfast rolls with custard, red wine.

There's no one in the checkout line, just a young girl behind the register wearing a multicolored, hand-knit scarf that reminds me of a Malibu boutique at Christmas. I unpack the basket, watch my items pass over the scanner, pay cash as the girl barely looks at me. I think about how Kris said- that this island makes things better. Perhaps she had already found some sort of resolution, found happiness here while riding a bike around Roche Harbor, having a beer on a run-down porch, walking the mushy trail along Lime Kiln Point. And then I wonder, if I do all those things, maybe the same will happen for me.

∽

Grace has lit what seems like every candle in the house. The curtains are open but the house is dim, the sky becoming overcast again. I kick the front door closed; my hands full of groceries. I smell magnolia and shaving cream. I call out hello and walk out onto the patio where Grace is sitting, legs crossed, her hair in a high pony tail and brochures cover her lap.

"I got some groceries, stuff for breakfast," I say.

"I wonder how many trips you average a week to that store," she says, smiling a little, teasing me. There's a light-heartedness, and it's a relief.

I nod instead of arguing or defending myself. She's right.

"Richard went out for a run," she says, examining the brochures. "Think he tried to wait for you."

The tide is in and our dock is barely visible. The trees look black, the air saturated, it feels like a storm.

Grace taps the brochures. "We should do something. Take Richard somewhere." She uncrosses her legs. "A group activity."

I nod. "Anything you think, I'm up for," I say, glad she's interested. I hope that she might find something she loves so much and consider staying longer.

"We can go horseback riding. Or fishing," she says and her eyes open really wide, and there is an enthusiasm there that I haven't seen in so long, one that used to be there between us during the times after Sam and I would fight and I'd end up at her house, sitting on her couch, staring out the tiny patio door at the lights below Mulholland. She'd grab my purse and keys, stand by the door and say, "Get up, Eva, we're going for a drink." Other times she'd show up on a set when I was filming in Los Angeles with cold In&Out Burgers and soggy fries and sit cross-legged on my trailer floor, telling me stories about her friends from UCLA. When she came to the house when Sam wasn't there, she'd drag me to her favorite restaurant up Topanga. I'd always get nauseous as she took the corners of the canyon road to fast. She'd look over at me and say, "Just close your eyes. We're almost there. It'll be so worth it."

She opens her MacBook and starts typing, probably researching places on the island. I feel the pang of missing her even though she's a few feet away. The closeness. Like sisters, or what I imagined a sibling to be. Maybe we were even closer. We didn't have the resentment that comes or builds with blood ties. We never competed for our parent's attention, fought over the front seat, thought a parent took one of us to more places than the other. And even though she was younger, and it kept us at a distance for a while, especially through my teenage years when I was protective, and lectured. I knew everything she didn't, telling her with a condescending tone. But as she reached her twenties, a change happened. We became friends, women trying to discover our way through uncertainty with a history, a connection that strengthened through each obstacle. When I married Sam and little cracks starting climbing the walls of our relationship; she started taking steps away from me, baby steps I didn't notice. Then her stride widened until I couldn't reach her, no matter how hard I tried.

"What do you think, Eva?" She turns her computer so I can see the HorseShu Ranch website. "We can do a private ride. Skip the group."

I nod. "Perfect," I say and smile. She's always planning, organizing. She makes excel spread sheets to plan birthday parties and vacations. A lot of the time I forget how much younger she is—she even seems older. She starts typing again and I'm reminded of when she came to visit me in Spain when I was filming. I was so tired on my days off, but she'd drag me out the door, start the ignition of our Fiat and say, "How could you even think of staying inside?" She'd drive me to town, make us walk, explore. She'd point out gray, grandiose cathedrals, ornate hotels and marble statues—always looking ahead of us and up. Every time we went through a crowd or walked through a parade, whistles blowing, boots stomping, she'd reach out for me, take my hand or link my arm.

I sit down in the chair next to her, watch as she reads something intensely. I fold the pamphlets. I take a quick breath "Are you okay with Richard being here?" I ask.

"Absolutely," she says, not looking at me. "Visitors are good. And he's like family, right?" Her cheeks flush, her lips press together.

I might believe her if I didn't know her so well. "If it bothers you, we should talk about it," I say. "I don't know how long he'll be here."

"It's all good, Eva." She stands and sets the computer on the chair. "I'm going to take a shower and get ready."

I want to tell her not to go. Does she think I came here to forget Sam and erase all the memories—forget completely and start anew with no trace of who I've known or who I've been? She brushes her hair out of her eyes and then walks towards the screen door. I know we can't keep up this tension, that it won't hold. Like water filling a house in a flood, rushing, rising steadily until it fills the insides, the pressure mounting, until the walls can't withstand it and everything collapses. It will be something small—someone leaving the milk out too long or erasing a show on the DVR that might cause the burst. And then we will say things we can't take back, snapping the last of our connection, casting an irremovable shadow over the best memories. Would she then leave, disappear, taking a huge part of my childhood with her.

She fumbles with the screen handle as if she's thinking about turning around, coming back. She stands there for a few seconds and I notice the scar on her neck, a few loose strands brushing against it. It's jagged, white and keloid. It reminds me of something I almost forgot. With Grace you can never really tell how or what she's feeling. Pain, discomfort, even pure joy—it's all hidden. I remember when she got the scar, she was eleven and Sam and I were seventeen. We didn't keep an eye on her as she made her way across the slippery rocks at the tide pools during low tide. Sam and I went too fast, too far ahead, him holding my hand, pulling me as we jumped from rock to rock. After a while, we looked back and she'd slipped and fallen backwards, her hands sprawled out, her head hanging forward. She never made a sound.

CHAPTER

THIRTEEN

Richard walks one pace ahead of me and closest to the street—always has since I've known him. I used to think it was because of his impeccable manners or it was some protective thing. He'd use his body as a natural shield to whatever could happen, leaving those behind or next to him safe. But as I got to know him, I realized that was only part of it. He was usually looking up, right, and left, scanning, as if being steps ahead would give him more time to take everything in—and if he had to stop, he wouldn't hold anyone up. He was looking at things most people don't notice. Bent branches, variations in cloud patterns, a part of a building that had been rebuilt, the unique features of someone that sets him or her apart, or the way light filters through shedding trees.

I keep my eyes focused on the back of his head as I try to keep up, my hands buried in soft pockets. I smile. We dressed so similar without meaning to do it. Columbia down jackets, black workout pants and running shoes with colorful thick tread. He stops abruptly and when I reach him, he gently tugs on one of my braids and smiles. I don't know what to do, so I adjust the knit beanie on my head. He nods and then continues on and we start the climb out of Roche Harbor.

For a while there are only clusters of trees around us, wet branches above us, and an overcast sky that makes it appear later in the day than it is. The morning sun not yet poking through.

"It's just ahead," I say, pointing to the entrance of the Sculpture Garden.

"Is Grace meeting us later this morning?" Richard asks. We have all fallen into a routine. Richard and I alternating making breakfast, Grace writing most of the day and then joining us at some point in the afternoon. Twice a week, Kris has been meeting up with us, showing us some part of the island, we haven't yet uncovered. "She might," I say keeping his pace. "If she finishes her chapter." We continue along the path and I think about the last three weeks, the morning walks or runs, evening boat rides, Grace on her computer in the late afternoons, Richard on his, or on the phone, his voice low from the office, me either in the kitchen trying a new recipe or reading a book, always near them, watching them work, feeling so far removed from a professional life.

"I'd like to take you two out to dinner tonight, if that's okay," Richard says. "Somewhere we can get dressed up."

"Yes, but dinner's my treat," I say. "It's the least I can do." He's done so much, coming here, staying longer than he planned, quietly urging me out of the house, keeping me moving, forward.

We come to a wheat grass field and scattered green pathways that lead up to various sculptures of artwork. A gray pond floats in the middle with barren trees encircling it. Bunched Douglas firs run the edge of the bank. Through them I can see a hint of the ocean and an outline of a nearby island.

"We go in here," I say, pressing on a large iron gate with black swirled cutouts and gold trim.

He opens it and waits for me to go through. Across the pond there's a man and woman huddled close together, arms draped around each other.

Richard takes the lead and we enter slowly. He stops at each sculpture or piece and we linger at what I take to be his favorites. I reach up and touch a bronze loon, its wings are spread. I feel the ridges on its body. Richard watches from a few feet away. When I turn back and look at him, he holds my gaze.

At the pond, a caged iron dragonfly protrudes from the water. The couple ahead of us walks across the small bridge towards the path that leads into the covering of trees.

Richard points down at a silver plaque among clovers and weeds. I read the inscription: *Will there be a place for me?*

"I like that one," Richard says.

"Me, too," I say.

We pass a stone buffalo and a smooth nude female sculpture arched on her toes, under a sun suspended from two poles. I bury my hands further in my coat.

"I missed you," he says quietly. "When you left L.A."

I look up at him, but he stares straight ahead at the sculpture, and stops walking.

"I got used to those afternoons at your place at the beach," he says. He adjusts his Dodger hat, and then pulls the bill down and his eyes are shadowed.

"I did, too," I say.

"I haven't been out to the beach since you left," he says.

"Those were nice afternoons," I answer, and think of the last one we had before I left. He'd showed up around 3 p.m., wearing a suit. He'd come from Westlake, from a lunch meeting at the Four Seasons. I was stretched out on the double chaise lounge on the second story deck, wrapped in a heavy wool throw, reading the *Life of Pi*. When the sliding door opened, I didn't turn. I knew it was him. He stood over me and set a bottle of wine down on the side table. "I thought you could use this," he'd said, loosening his silk tie. "Looks like we both could use it," I'd answered. The banter made me feel normal. It was easy, natural. He'd smiled slyly and said he'd go get some glasses. I'd reached up and grabbed his hand, and he took it and squeezed.

"How's it been going for you up here?" Richard asks, pulling me from my thoughts. "What do you think now that time's gone by?"

I look down and trace circles in the dirt with my shoe. "It's been good to get away," I say.

"Starting to feel any different?" he asks.

I nod, bite my lip and can't help but notice his tone sounds softer, hopeful.

Both of us turn when we hear voices. Without thinking, I take a step closer to him. He clears his throat as the couple comes toward us. Their arms are linked, their bodies so close, so comfortable; their limbs move together in unison.

Richard grabs my hand and pulls me over to where he's standing. The wind is picking up, there's a chill off the water. The couple passes us, saying hello and nodding politely. Richard squeezes my hand as if to say, no big deal, people don't care here, this is a different world. He laces his fingers through mine, and I remember this was our signal so long ago, when we first became friends, after Isabelle split for New York when he took her place next to me at a crowded premiere or a loud, noisy charity benefit. It was a reminder to breathe, stop worrying, and let the negative thoughts go.

As I watch the couple walk away, I remember how when I was younger, I used to let go of his hand quickly, as soon as I felt comfortable—but I don't now. I want to stay here, exactly like this. Instead of silk or Italian wool, it's our feather jackets that rub against each other. My hip fitting into his side, watching our breath in the air.

"This is my favorite part of the trail," I say as we go on. I point to where artists have placed their work amongst the trees: a carved bench made of bleached driftwood and a hanging translucent metal sheet from a large branch.

White moss covers most everything around us and it looks like powdery frost. The path tapers off into weeds and slopes down to the water lapping against the shore. Richard reads every plaque aloud while I sit on a bench between two trees and listen to his voice, deep and interested. Eventually, it becomes the only sound, mixed with smells of wet pine and burnt ocean air.

We must have been here for a couple of hours; the sun is coming out creating a rose tint amongst the haze. It's getting colder and I tuck my hands under my knees. Richard skips a few rocks over the water. I keep waiting for other people to come by but they don't.

"Ready?" I watch the rings on the water from where the skipped stones touched and disappeared.

"Sure," he says walking over to where I'm seated on the bench. He stops in front of me; he reaches out his hand to help me up.

He's so close and I smell shampoo and coffee. Tiny waves slap against floating beached logs. I take his hand, but neither of us move. I can't meet his gaze. I inch forward on the bench and lean in towards him, rest my cheek on his stomach, and feel the padding from his jacket as he breathes in deep. I'm afraid if I make another movement, something will change.

He shifts his weight and I look up at him.

He runs his hand down my face, cups my chin. His fingers move along my jaw, holding me there. His brow creased, he looks concerned or as if he's doing something wrong or fighting something he knows he can't help.

I begin to stand.

"Let's head back," he says, taking a step back.

His movement is so quick and jarring. I feel tears coming. "Yep, it's getting late," I say.

He shoves his hands in his pockets, looks ahead and starts up the path. I count to three, get up, wait for him to stop and reach out his hand or explain what's happening or what just happened. But he never does.

As we walk back, I stay a few yards behind and I feel something shifting. For the last fifteen years I've never had the inclination to lean into Richard, rest against him or to wait for his lead. Did something start in the sculpture garden or did it start way before? And how long ago. I've started to do what I told myself I never would; let myself remember things, sounds, smells, words that remind me of the past and Sam's death and my premiere. I'm not fighting it anymore. When the memories come, wash over me, they're no longer drowning, suffocating, debilitating. Maybe with that acceptance, the surrender, it's allowed other things and people to enter.

Richard turns around and motions for me to catch up.

I run to catch up and know all that's happened to me. I have no choice but to believe it now. And everything that it's left in its wake is right in front of me, around me nudging my senses back to life.

CHAPTER
FOURTEEN

The dock attendant helps Grace up the steps to the pontoon plane and as he lets go of her hand, just before she ducks inside, she turns and waves to me. I watch her take the seat next to the pilot; her green parka casts a lemon light in the cockpit. I get back into my car but don't start the engine until they begin to take off. I close my eyes and listen to the loud rattle and the whining as they lift into the air. I'd asked her to take the ferry or the small commuter jet. She shook her head and said she liked the experience in the nine-seater prop plane. Someday she would be flying one, off on research trips deep into the Puget Sound.

I drive back to the house, the sun setting on the other side of the island and I miss her already. The opposite of what I thought I'd feel this soon. I was determined to believe that her returning to Seattle was what we needed; a break, the time apart easing the tension. I had no idea I would feel an instant separation—with each mile I felt the pull-away of the familiar and consistency. What happens when she has to go back to school and her life completely? When she goes, will everything go with her?

My cell phone beeps. The text is from Kris; she ran out of salad dressing and asks if Richard and I could pick some up on our way over for dinner. I force my thoughts away from Grace's departure and tell myself I have to remember the Vinaigrette. I'm suddenly nervous if Richard's going to be ready to go when I get home, that my outfit, leggings, a sweater, knee high boots is overkill for a Thursday evening at a white Cape Cod style house facing Vancouver Island.

Richard's standing outside when I pull up to the house and I smile as he opens the car door—a rush of cocoa butter drifts through and I feel something shift. A reality sets in as he puts on his seat belt, his face clean shaven with a lotion glow. Grace is gone, there is nobody with us anymore. It's him and me.

I watch Kris standing over Richard, refilling his wine glass, talking about commercial island properties. He listens to her intensely and her hand is placed so gently on her stomach, gripping the Merlot bottle in the other. Everything she does is with ease, natural, everyone around her feels it, gathers in, like trying to get closer to the crackling, intense warmth of a fire. She asks if I want some more wine and without looking down stops pouring at just the right moment. I wonder if she had to teach herself all this ease, or if it's simply instinctual, or an accidental process, something that arrives as you settle into a simple, satisfied time of life.

I find myself wanting to touch my stomach, but I don't. I look down, take a quick breath. Kris's calmness, her contentment—I remember feeling that way when I was first pregnant, before anyone knew. For those few weeks, I felt protective, strong. Like the child I couldn't see or feel was willing me to start taking care of myself and then her.

Richard takes a bite of salad, listening to her talk. Every once in a while, he looks at me out of the corner of his eye. Maybe he notices me studying her. I can't hold his gaze so I keep focused on Kris, the outline of her stomach, her peachy skin glow in the dimmed dining room light. Her shoulders back and her gaze soft and when she listens to Richard's comments, her brows furrow gently revealing a deep line. Being around her has made me realize something I could never articulate when I was newly pregnant. You can never love someone enough, and their love will never be enough to give up a child, especially if you know you were meant to have one.

"What are you guys doing tomorrow?" Kris asks, settling back in her chair at the head of the table.

"Not sure," Richard answers quickly. He must know and sense I'm lost, deep in thought about something I can't yet explain.

"I thought I'd take Richard to Kilm Point or maybe go over to Orcas for dinner," I say, pulling myself from my trance, my voice soft.

"That sunset on the north side of Orcas is beyond incredible," she says. "You should go for a couple days."

"Is Ryan working tomorrow night?" I ask. "You could join us."

She nods. "He's on a 48-hour shift. Overtime." She looks around the room. "I miss him when he's gone. Especially now."

How quickly and easily Kris and I have become friends. What started with walks in the morning, turned to a few trips to the nursery to replant her garden, then afternoon visits and introductions to a few people. She's never asked me questions, probed me to open up about anything or pumped me about films or people I know. Our relationship has developed on the here and now, the present. It's all made me feel at home, as if she were my greeter at the pathway to this new life, her soothing voice and steady energy easing me in and forward.

"How much longer are you here?" Kris says to Richard as she leans back in her chair.

He takes a long sip from his wine. "I think another few days."

"You should stay longer," I say, and I look at Kris, surprising myself with the honesty. She nods and smiles.

He pauses before setting his glass back down. "We'll see," he says.

"You should definitely extend your trip," Kris says, nodding. "There are so many other places Eva needs to show you."

She's right, there are places I need to show him, even see for myself. I stand, reach for the plates, and start to clear the table.

"Sit," Kris says. "I'll get this all later."

Richard stands too, pushes up the sleeves of his sweater and picks up his glass. "We insist on helping."

It's the second time he's said, "we." I can't help but think about all those years ago, the couple of dates he and Isabelle went on. I watched as they left the house together, going to a dinner party, or a new restaurant in Santa Monica, her dressed in a black silk dress, or tight jeans. He would open her car door, place his hand on the small of her back. I try to push the images out of my head, feeling a pit in my stomach.

I set the plates down.

"It's late," Kris says. "You guys should get going before it gets absolutely pitch black on that road."

I nod, not sure what to say or feel, confused. Part of me wants to stay here, not sure if I should go with Richard back to the house or what we're doing or why I encouraged him to stay. Am I jealous suddenly of my mother and Richard, of something that almost happened between them almost twenty years ago? Can he separate me from Isabelle or am I a reminder of something familiar?

Kris puts an arm around my waist and urges me to the door, as if she senses what's going on in my head. I hug her, and hold on.

Richard drives slower than usual. I focus on the dark shadows of trees that border the road, white bursts of light from oncoming cars.

"What were you thinking about at dinner?" he asks. I feel his arm resting on the armrest, inches from me.

"How things used to be," I say. "Could have been."

"What things?" his voice drops lower. I glance at him. His gaze is intense, serious.

"Being pregnant."

He slows the car even more and I look ahead at the dark road and then back over at him. His profile looks silver, and his face softer, younger. He takes a deep breath but his expression doesn't change. "You made the right choice to try," he says. "To have the baby."

"A lot of good it did," I say, surprised that it doesn't hurt so intensely to talk about it with him.

"You made a decision on your own. Apart from what he thought or any influence. I hadn't really seen that from you for a long time."

I put my elbow on the armrest next to his. He doesn't flinch when we touch. "How come you've never said that before?"

"I should have," he says. "I didn't think you were ready to discuss it. You were really shut down. No one could reach you."

I feel the thick cotton of his sweater against my bare forearm. We pass some houses and then a break in the trees—only a dark field, the water beyond, like black ruptured glass.

"Everything's starting to feel easier," I say. "That's what I was thinking about tonight at dinner, too."

"I think they have been for some time. I could see that when I first got here," he says. He shifts his body in the seat and he reaches over and takes my hand.

"Grace gets back in a week," I say, closing my fingers around his hand. I feel my heart quicken.

"I know." He makes a left and pulls the car into the driveway.

"Will you be gone before that?" I ask. He eases on the brake and the car stops but neither of us move.

"I have to see if I can move things around. I need to make some calls to L.A. Check on things. I've stayed way longer than I intended. Things are probably chaos there."

He reaches over with his other hand and puts the car in park and shuts it off. He keeps a grip on my hand and I wait for him to make a move to get out.

"I heard from Isabelle today," he says.

I wince when he says her name, afraid he's going to tell me she's wondering what he's doing here, why he's been here so long.

He stares straight ahead. "She asked me how you're doing. Says you guys have been emailing but that's about it."

I keep waiting for him to turn towards me, look at me, convinced I'll be able to tell from his expression how he feels.

"Did she ask you what you're doing here?" I say, studying the front door of the house, the circular wedges in the wood.

"That never even came up," he says. "You know how your mother is, keeps it light."

"Even with you?" I ask.

"Especially with me," he says, smiling. "She and I hadn't really had a conversation in years." He shifts in his seat. "The only reason we're still in contact is because of you."

I nod, don't say anything else, don't challenge him or ask any more about my mother. He runs his hand through his hair.

"You should reach out to her, Eva. A little more."

"I know," I say.

His palm is starting to get clammy and I loosen my grip. His arm has to be at an uncomfortable angle but he gives no hint of it. I'm afraid if I move too much or open the door, whatever this is might disappear. This connection, this feeling. Coming from a new friend's house, an old friend driving me is not a huge occurrence, but I feel the happiness in the everyday. It almost makes me want to begin to hope for what's to come.

FIFTEEN

Because of Sam I'm used to sleeping in a big bed, a California King I still have, that he was overly attached to. It sits in our house on the beach, thousands of miles from me. The mattress has one side more indented than the other and seams torn on the left bottom corner. No matter which way I stretched on that mattress, or turned—I could never fill it up once he was gone. No amount of pillows ever warmed the bottom sheet. The coldness beneath me sometimes woke me in the night, just like tonight.

I sit up in this queen-sized bed, the strap of my nightgown slipping down my shoulder and I look out the window at Pearl Island, the dark houses that line the edge, the dinghies bobbing in front, anchored to the bottom of a stormy ocean.

I feel the weight of the blankets on me, the duvet slipping off this much smaller bed. I think about the day Sam and I moved to the Malibu house two years ago before he died—when we drove the forty plus miles in his pick-up truck from our hilltop cottage to our ivory beach house on stilts. The huge mattress was in the back, tied down, plastic wrap ripping loose. He insisted we take it with us. "We don't need to buy a custom, hand stitched new mattress like the designer wanted," he had said. "This one will remind us who we are, who we were, where we came from."

I flip on the light, think about why I fought him so hard about throwing away that mattress. It was never about the prestige of new furniture from a design house off Robertson Boulevard. I think it was that I believed a new house, a new bed, new everything would be a fresh start, close a distance, erase unhappy years, un-do words we screamed at one another. Or help us forget that life in town; when at some point he started checking out women who passed us in huge black sunglasses and bandage dresses, and how his expression went blank and his gaze drifted off when people asked him what he did for a living at parties with flashing bulbs and blue-lit vodka fountains. I convinced myself that a new place filled with things we didn't recognize, that smelled new, of white paint, would make us different somehow.

A single light is on in the kitchen as I come down the stairs. I don't know the time but it must be two, three in the morning. Outside, the ocean looks black. The dishes still in the sink make me miss Grace. She had kept an immaculate kitchen, shiny clean tiles and white walls, glasses placed in cupboards in neat rows, coffee that seemed to always be freshly made, with syrupy smells from something always cooking.

"It's not as clean without Grace here," Richard says from behind me.

His voice surprises me, it's lower, or deeper and I feel my fist close, nails wedged in my palm.

"I was just noticing," I say, attempting to sound casual even though his shirt's off and all I can think about is how my face had rested against his stomach in the Sculpture Garden, his flannel soft on my cheek and everything smelled liked crushed leaves. "I have a feeling she's met someone, or has had someone in her life but hasn't said," I say. "Her voice sounds different when I talk to her on the phone. She's happier. Lighter."

He opens the refrigerator as I lean against the sink, look out, focus on the plastic owl nailed to the corner of the porch railing. "I wonder if she's coming back."

Richard selects a carton of something, pulls out a chair and sits. His hair looks tousled, his flannel pajama bottoms are wrinkled at the bottom.

"She'll be back," he says, taking a bite of left-over pasta. "I think she's been with someone for a while, or it's been on and off."

Taking a glass from the shelf, I try and pinpoint the exact moment things started to shift between us and why the other day I felt it was okay to lean into him, in such an intimate way, after so many hours and years of us talking about weather and scripts and new restaurants on 3rd Street in Hollywood.

I turn to look at him. "I've been clueless about her love life," I say. "Or is it self-absorbed?"

"Probably a little of both," he says, smiling slightly as he takes another bite.

"I guess I haven't been there much for anyone," I say and don't really know what to do or feel about this realization. I'd always been the person who was there for everybody else or faked it well. Taking on everyone's burdens, loads, feeling the same pain they felt, or thinking I did. Somehow along the way I stopped being able to differentiate my problems from theirs, taking everything on my shoulders until when my own sadness arrived, I had no room left to handle it, to carry it. Until my feet, and knees buckled under the weight.

I smell cold Chow Mein, leftovers from hours ago, when we'd eaten in front of the T.V., Richard in the chunky leather chair, me on the couch, the news dragging on, us making random comments because we weren't sure what to say, to do.

"Couldn't sleep?" I ask, changing the subject. I'm still standing in the same spot, an empty glass in my hand.

"I drank too much coffee after you went to bed," Richard says. "I was up for a while talking to Bill," he says.

"Let me guess, problems with the edits on the first episode?"

He nods. "It's always the most difficult."

"When do they start writing the next season?"

"April," he says, setting down his fork.

"That's not for a while," I say, wondering, if he stayed another month, what would happen.

"I know," he says, standing.

I take a small step. "The two of us here," I say. "This makes me think of when Isabelle left for New York and I stayed with you."

He clears his throat. "That was a long time ago," he says finally, coming towards me. "You were a kid." He looks at me and I smile.

"I'm not now," I say.

He stops in front of me, a carton in his hand, and I realize he needs to throw it away. I move quickly out of the way, sit down in the nearest chair at the table.

He throws the food away, then turns around. "Things are different now, a lot has changed."

My eyes wander around the room and I know he's right. It feels like I wouldn't recognize the two of us back then. I was fifteen pounds heavier, hair cropped to my shoulders, my face was rounder, my hair was platinum blonde, it took me awhile to look people in the eyes; my heart was beating on my sleeve. He was a thirty-something up and coming producer, his first T.V. show picked up, he was just starting to buy furniture from Restoration Hardware and take the women he was dating to New York City or Sonoma for the weekend.

"Are we still having dinner in town tomorrow, meeting your friend?" he asks.

"Think so," I say. I'll call Kris to confirm in the morning."

He nods, walks behind my chair.

I don't turn around but imagine his face, calm eyes looking ahead, biting his top lip, the way he does right before he says something important. The dark room makes his skin deeper brown. I feel his hand on my shoulder, fingers tracing my collarbone.

I take a deep breath when his fingertips press hard on my skin. "We *are* different people now, Richard," I say, and don't know if it's a hopeful statement or a question or if I need reassurance.

He steps closer, his other hand rests gently on the nape of my neck, slowly moving, and I can smell a hint of a lavender candle blown out hours before. He lets his hand rest on my check and I lean into it, my face feeling small in his palm. My eyes close, I push back my chair to get up. He lets go.

"It's late," he says. "Get some sleep."

As he walks away, all I can do is stare outside, focus on the pink faded windsock that flies near the window. The glass rattles from the wind, the trees appear to be bending.

A door closes upstairs and I have no idea what to do or think. Should I leave on the first ferry out in the morning, go somewhere safe, before something happens? Should I go upstairs after him, ask him why he pulled away or keeps pulling away or should I take the cushions off the patio furniture before the rain starts? Maybe I call Isabelle and Grace and tell them that I can almost get through an entire day now without thinking of Sam, or my guilt, the past, or our wedding rings I left at home in a safe. What I'd really like to share with someone is that for a while, in this kitchen, when Richard touched me, I couldn't remember a history or past of any kind.

I pull the car into the garage, glance over at the baby present in the passenger seat and I feel strong. The pink glittery box sitting next to me maybe a symbol, a rite of passage, a reminder that things get easier, and no matter if we're ready for it, time moves us on. I think about how somewhere, at some time, I don't know when it happened, but it did—I stopped hearing the name I picked for my child-to-be. It used to play again and again in my head, over and over. Like a song accidentally stuck on repeat on iTunes and you're too tired to get up and change it. So, you just let it go until it drives you insane. And then after that stopped, I became able to pronounce words and names I used to not be able to speak aloud. I began to imagine the pitch, the sweetness of Sam's voice when he said, *Eva Marie*. I began to let myself remember rooms filled with pictures and things that I left behind. When did it happen, when did it become easier? It could have started in yoga class, lying on my mat with my limbs folded, muscles shaky and clothes sweaty after class, the intense heat in the room extracting any impurity or imperfection in me. Or perhaps it was waiting for Kris for a morning walk, watching as she walked towards our meeting place, putting on her sweatshirt, struggling to fit it over her expanding stomach, smiling at me. Maybe it was during the hours of three and four in the morning when I'd wake because a fisherman was trolling too close to shore, trees shadowing through the bedroom curtains, the smell of pines drifting in through the vents. Whenever it was, that's when I began to understand what Isabelle meant right before she moved to New York all those years ago. The words she'd whispered to me when she crawled into my bed after a late night out, the softness of her fur coat or silk blouse, brushing against my hair and cheek, her vodka breath saying, "The good things in life don't happen until you invite them. Until there is no more fight left."

I close the garage door and wonder, have I stopped fighting the newness that's everywhere? I glance at the baby gift again, a hand-knit sweater and matching cap picked up at one of the boutiques in town, for Kris's daughter to wear someday. How easy it was to hand it to the cashier, to watch as she folded the tiny arms and covered it with tissue paper. There was no panic or fear that I'd expected.

Richard's car is gone and part of me is relieved. I'd left early, before he woke, managed to stay in town for hours—at the museum, and the nursery, picking out new flowers for the garden. What would I have said after our middle of the night run-in in the kitchen? How would it have been over breakfast, both of us staring out at something on the horizon, milk and cereal spilling as we ate without looking?

I open the front door, go to the kitchen, set down the bags on the table, notice all the things from stores that I probably don't need. And despite all my efforts to distract myself, yoga, errands, trinkets, I can still feel the sensation of him standing behind me last night as I sat in this chair, his voice so low and calm above me. As he walked away, his bare feet padding on wood floor.

I check to see if there are any messages on my cell phone, still no word from Grace. I close my eyes and picture her as I always do when I'm not with her; a place she is happiest. Like the Pike Market on a Sunday, wearing her mother's favorite mauve Italian print scarf tied around her neck, or somewhere off the Sound, knee-deep in water, wearing an inside-out thermal.

I miss her. I miss the Grace, I knew her to be before all this happened. I unpack things from the bags and wonder how I could have forgotten how young she is. Should I encourage her to stay put in Seattle, cut her free from me, from this, from the memory of her brother? I look around at the kitchen, the living room, and the sofas with velvety throws, white sheer curtains, and white orchids in white vases.

The front door closes quietly and I call out hello before Richard sees me. When he doesn't reply, I go to the bags on the table, rustle through them, look for something else to put away, tell myself to act normal.

He walks in, stops in the doorway. His parka is still on.

"Hey," he says.

Something in his tone, his posture is different. His shoulders are stiff. Something's changed. For the better or worse I don't know. "Are you leaving?" I ask, trying not to sound anxious. Because that's what scares me and relieves me all at the same time.

He shakes his head while I try and concentrate on what I'm doing, hide that I'm panicked, heart racing.

"Where've you been all day?" he asks, still not taking off his jacket. He rattles the keys in his hand.

"Why don't you take of your coat," I say, unpacking something else, trying not to let my hands shake, not ready for him to leave.

"You didn't answer your cell," he says and I can't remember the last time I heard him sound annoyed.

"I didn't have it with me," I say.

He walks to the refrigerator, gets a beer.

I wait until he opens it, tell myself when the cap comes off, I'll ask. "Are going back?"

"To L.A?" He takes a long sip. Shakes his head. "Not yet."

I take a deep breath. "Where were you?" I ask as he sits down.

"In town," he says.

"So was I," I say.

He picks at the label on the beer bottle. He seems to do this for minutes. "I was checking the ferry times at the dock," he says finally.

I want to ask him a million questions but I'm afraid I'll scare him, scare myself. So, I wait.

"I thought I'd go over, check out Orcas and maybe stay a few nights." He takes another sip. "Cascade Bay Resort," he says just as I'm about to ask where he plans to stay.

"It's beautiful there," I whisper.

"The guy at the ticket counter said it's pretty empty this time of the year," Richard says.

I stand slowly, my eyes meet his, and I hold his gaze before I go to the refrigerator.

"Come with me," he says.

I squeeze the door handle—I was right, something's different. It's not an invitation to breakfast, or dinner at Geoffrey's on a cliff in the north part of Malibu, or a matinee in the worn-down theatre on Wilshire. The things we did for years. How could I possibly go? After everything? He went on dates with my mother for a brief time, maybe even pined for her when she moved, the only woman who ever rejected him. Does he look at me and see her? How could he not, the shape of our eyes are the same. He knew me before Sam, during Sam, and now after Sam. He never told me to leave him like everyone else, he never insinuated it by saying, "You're young, you can find someone else." He never told me not to marry him, he never screamed at me: how could you not want more for yourself? He never said things like, I told you so, or I always knew it wouldn't work. Why? He watched me curled up in that hospital room, a year after Sam's death, mascara running down my face and smeared red lipstick, refusing, afraid to look him in the eye. Can he see me, now, for who I am or who I will become? Or does he see me, all disjointed? When he looks at me are the memories and situations, all the good and the bad, all the years separated in fragments, like jigsaw puzzle pieces on a table waiting to be connected, to make something whole?

"We were supposed to have dinner with Kris and her husband tonight," I finally respond, because I can't say anything else.

"Turn around."

I do as he tells me and he sits up straighter, both hands folded on the table. "Is it important I come with you to dinner?" he asks.

I can't look at him; my eyes drift to the hallway, the jackets, scarves and purses hanging on a wood coat tree by the door. I shake my head, "No. Go ahead to the island. You should at least see some different places while you're still up here." I say quietly. I feel how weak I am, how much I'm disappointing him, and myself.

He nods for a few seconds, his mouth closed. He stands, pushes his chair back, scratching the floor. I watch, unable to move as he puts his jacket on, and prepares to go out into a storm. "I'll see you later then, Eva," he says. "The last boats in half an hour."

I nod. "See you in a few days," I say. He hasn't shaved, the hair coming through on his face is sprinkled with grey. His eyes look bluer and clear.

He walks down the hallway, stops and picks up a bag. I sit down at the table because my legs are unsteady. I want to say all the things I'm supposed to. Like, stop, Richard don't go, wait for me. But I picture Isabelle, the last time I saw her, at the airport months ago, how her hand grabbed mine. I picture Grace's eyes filling up at Sam's funeral, her mouth opening as tears spilled over, but no sound escaping as Sam's ashes blew into to the ocean.

Richard opens the front door. "Your mother called me again asking about you. Call her."

And then the door closes hard.

CHAPTER
SIXTEEN

Kris hands me a cup of something I know I won't drink. My stomachs in knots. Sitting down across from me on the patio, she wraps a woven blanket tightly around her shoulders. The sun's setting, red and hazel smears across the sky. Kris and Ryan's whaler bobs just off shore, a part of the cover loose and flapping in the wind. She smooths her hair and I wonder when I started trusting her so completely. Did it happen in the last hour? It might have been when she opened her front door wider tonight when she saw it was me, gestured for me to come in without asking questions, touched the side of my face and said, "Be right back, I'll get you something warm to drink?" I don't remember driving over here, but just knew this was where I wanted to go—this white cottage-style house with white flowers, white cushions, dark, wood furniture that looked as if flown in from a balmy country far away.

"Ryan's going to be late," she says, crossing her legs. "We have a while to talk."

The cushion beneath me feels cold. I pull my jacket tighter around me and realize I'd grabbed Richard's extra jacket on my way out the door. The sleeves are too long, and I tuck my hands in them. I used to take Sam's without thinking. "I'm sorry I just showed up," I say. "Early."

She looks at me shakes her head, smiles as if to say don't be ridiculous.

"I couldn't sit in that house anymore. Richard left," I say. "Everyone's gone."

"Back to L.A.?" she asks, her voice calm, as if she isn't surprised.

I shake my head. "He went to Orcas for a few days." I picture him sitting at a table at Friday Harbor House waiting for them to start boarding. Fresh fish on his plate, red wine looking purple against the dim lights—glancing every once a while at the view. The water appearing darker as the sun sets. "He asked me to go with him," I say.

She nods and I keep waiting for her to be shocked or surprised. I wait for her to say something and watch as she picks up her mug with both hands, takes a slow sip. I look away because she doesn't take her eyes off me and it feels like she's disappointed somehow.

"I said I needed to come to dinner, here," I say, focusing on the ocean.

"And you want me to tell you that you did the right thing," she says.

Her hair is curling from the heaviness of the fog rolling in. She's so relaxed, comfortable, everything I wish I felt. "He's my friend, he has been for so long. You don't understand."

"The man I met at dinner the other night wasn't your friend, darlin'."

I start to say I don't agree, but instead I look inside her house, at the table we were all seated at just a week ago. There were plates of lobster, greens, melting butter on bread. I watched as Kris told a story, while Ryan sipped a cocktail never taking his eyes off her, leaning back in his chair. Candles flickered between dishes and bottles of wine. Richard and I made eye contact as Kris laughed; a lasting look between us and then Richard nodded. I'd held his glance as long as I could.

"You don't understand," I say again.

"Go," she says.

"Things are finally getting better between Isabelle and me and Grace seems to be starting to get past things. I'm feeling better," I say as my voice trails off.

"Go," she says again, taking another sip from her mug.

I shake my head.

"You're afraid that your mother and Grace will be angry or think you're making a mistake?"

"Yes," I say, embarrassed.

"I think you underestimate them," Kris says.

I look down at Richard's jacket, the way it hangs on me, loose but warm. "What if it changes everything?"

"What if it does?" she asks.

I close my eyes. "I don't think I'm ready for it. And he's not that encouraging, doesn't come right out and say what he wants." I think of Sam. How his green eyes would slant when he was happy, or the beautiful cone-shaped scar on his back that my hand would always rest or find at some point in the night. The day he'd got that cut was so warm and humid. When he wiped out on a wave, the fin of his surfboard sliced through his wetsuit, deep. He'd came out of the water, peeled it off slowly, and as I helped him up the hill, his warm blood rubbed against my forearm. After I'd settled him in the passenger seat, he'd said, tenderly, "I can't make it without you." I'd shut the door and ran back to the nearby aloe plant—picked some leaves, knowing he'd need them later, during the healing process.

Kris puts her hand on her stomach; it rests there under the curve. "If you don't go, things will still change. Either way."

"I don't know how I feel," I say. "I mean he's my mother's ex for Christ's Sake." I bite my lip when I hear the word *mother* come out of my mouth. When was the last time I'd said it?

"Hardly," she says. "From what you've told me, they went out on a few dates, three? Twenty years ago? I mean yes, it's a little awkward. But I think you're reaching for something."

I shake my head. "I guess when I really think about it, he's just Richard, my friend, someone who's always been there. But lately . . ."

"You feel like you just met," she says.

I look in her eyes, "Exactly." I realize that I've been curious, trying to discover things about him, like who he was before he met us, why he hasn't married yet, why he's quiet and always seems to be on the brink of saying something but holds back. What does it mean when his right leg bounces sometimes when we talk? Who were the women he's been dating recently, who has he deeply loved?

"What are you thinking?" she asks.

I don't know how long it's been quiet between us, foghorns moaning every few minutes. "I just can't to do it, Kris." It's all I can say.

"Okay. Why?"

I imagine trying to tell Grace that I've moved on from her brother, and Grace turning her back on me, taking the last connection to Sam. I hear myself telling Isabelle, then hearing her say, "You're doing it again, you chose wrong!" and disconnecting the call. Or would Richard tell me I'm not ready, that I still need to grieve. Would he leave for L.A., go back to a life I don't know anymore, our friendship going with him. Worse, he might tell me he doesn't feel the same way or he's on the fence with no answer in sight. Or if he did say he wanted to try, what would I do then? Does that thought of going to meet him allow me to start to want things? Long for things? Imagine things? What it would be like being with someone who truly loved me and knew me, someone who knew about the little things? Does it start to allow me to picture a life that I thought wasn't in the cards for me? Is that the scariest of all?

The front door closes and we both turn as Ryan comes out to join us. He places a hand on her cheek and kisses her, sits and takes her hand, rests it in his lap.

"Hi, baby." Kris smiles.

"Is Richard coming over?" he asks. I watch as she strokes his arm, her fingers tracing the ridges of his corduroy jacket.

"He went over to check out Orcas for a few days," I say and stand, not wanting to have the conversation about Richard anymore. Kris looks up at me as if to say, this discussion's not over. I think I can go to Orcas and then I think, I can't.

I check my watch, seven forty-five, 20 minutes until the last ferry.

We grab the mugs and Kris lets the blanket slip off her and into the chair. Ryan puts his hand on Kris's waist as he follows her in the door. She laughs at something he whispers.

I walk along the dock and wait to board the ferry for Orcas Island. My thoughts linger on last night, coming home from Kris's, standing in the entryway of my house, spotting the white envelope on my kitchen table, almost glowing in the darkness. I walked slowly towards it, saw my name in bold letters, underlined twice. A ticket was inside for the today's four p.m. ferry to Orcas along with a note:

I should have said more to convince you.
Change your mind. Join me.
—Richard

I'd texted Kris, telling her exactly what I'd found. A few minutes later, a message came back: "*Get yourself on that ferry.* I will pick you up at 3:15 pm and drive you there." I'd laughed but trusted the words, believed she could see the bigger picture, or had faith in something I didn't.

That note, Richard's scribbled handwriting, the closest to direct he's gotten propelled me, changed my mind, and now it keeps me walking forward, up the steps of the boat when I want to turn around, go home.

I take my seat up front, where there's no one. Now, late afternoon, the light's fading, the trees on the surrounding islands are a darker green. Fog rises off the water as we make our way out of Friday Harbor. I breathe deep. Salt water, diesel fumes, a nearby boat blows its horn and everyone turns.

People sit behind me and I don't turn, just listen to their heavy accents, from somewhere in Eastern Europe. It dawns on me—it was Richard who kept me going that day at the funeral, the strength I leaned against, his sturdiness I tapped into. He was there, not saying much, not chiming in as Grace, Isabelle and Russ threw opinions and lectures and schedules at me. He never pushed, needed, or asked for things from me. He made arrangements he knew I couldn't: renting the house up here, closing the house up in Malibu, making reservations for bike rentals, fishing trips, or food to be delivered. He gave me room while maintaining his own busy life, but making time somehow to be in mine. I must have known this, or noticed all along, felt it, been drawn it. That's why I'm going to Orcas, that's what packed my bag, got me out the door. All the moments with Richard have been quietly undoing fear and loss and all the things that paralyze me, like removing the thread, strand by strand, of a tightly sewn garment.

CHAPTER
SEVENTEEN

From: Gracie <h2oSeattleG@gmail.com>
Sent: Thursday, October 20. 2:41 AM
To: mbu.house123@gmail.com
Subject: Things

Eva,

I'm sorry I've been so out of touch, or not in touch enough
(I have been swamped and totally consumed at school) and
I wanted to send a note, say hi and that I miss you. I miss the
island house and especially that first sip of morning coffee,
bundled up, in our deck chairs.

There is a lot that is hard for me to say… a lot that is hard to
talk about when I'm with you. And I am so torn, wanting to be
there with you, for you, and needing to finish this/ my degree/
see it through. Even though it's super painful at times to be
together, because everything it drudges up, to have to
reconcile and look, stare down the hurt that my brother caused
you—it is such comfort to be with the only other person in the
world that understands.

Just all of it. The years, and childhood, intertwine us. And no matter what has happened, or will happen, we are sisters.

I hope that you will continue to explore that beautiful island, the people and I believe that whatever unfolds. It's supposed to be.

Until I get back, just know that I am over here, rooting for you, for me.

~Grace

CHAPTER

EIGHTEEN

Years ago, Richard told me to always trust the lows, the hard times in life—to not fight them. "They're part of it," he'd said. "You have to sit with them, lean in," he'd continued. "Or else there's no way you'll ever truly recognize or appreciate the flipside."

I remember we were on the phone, I was sipping on a Stella warm from the mini-bar fridge, my iPhone on the bedside table, his voice coming through the speakerphone in a patchy, lower pitch. The Chicago lights were a lemony blur outside my hotel room. It was late, I couldn't sleep, worried about a scene we had to re-do the next morning and I hadn't heard from Sam in four days.

"The flipside?" I'd asked after a long pause.

"The flipside is satisfaction," he'd answered.

I can still hear his tone, the sound of his voice that night as my cab pulls up to the Cascade Bay Inn on Orcas Island. It was steady, calm, but firm. As if he knew, or had a hunch something was coming —that I'd need his words to carry me through, eventually.

The driver puts the cab in park, and opens my door, almost in one smooth motion. I step out, breathe in. The air is damp and refreshing, a woven blend of saltwater and oak moss. The old inn was a converted Victorian mansion. Kris said it belonged to a ship builder in the early 1800s who built it for his wife.

I walk up the grand steps and at the top, I turn around to see if the cabs still there. He'd quietly driven off and I know I have no choice. I have to go in. I think of Grace's email, that came through just before I left. Her reflection, honesty, the hope for us—got me up, out the door. And her words: *whatever unfolds, it's supposed to be.* I take a step forward.

The entrance is lit by ivory candles flickering inside mosaic hurricanes and the fireplace in the lounge area casts off a soft glow. Large bay windows run the perimeter with panoramic views of the cove. In the distance, the Strait of San Juan de Fuca is sprinkled with chains of floating land backlit by the Olympic Mountains.

The dark burgundy carpets deepen the color of the wood furniture and the wall paneling has been recently restored to preserve its original ambiance. A tall woman stands behind the reception desk and I scan the lounge as she finishes up a phone call. A few people sit in the large, open room drinking wine from oversized glasses in front of the marble fireplace. Leather loveseats are angled in front of round tables and crystal chandeliers hang from the ceiling, giving off dainty pale light.

Richard stands when he sees me, and sets down his glass carefully. He smiles as he walks over. I don't answer when the receptionist asks, can I help you, Miss? Her eyes squint as if she thinks she recognizes me. My eyes are locked on Richard, and I'm unable to read him. He has no expression and his gaze is steady. I tighten the grip on the handle of my bag as he gets closer and then he kisses my cheek, his hand rests on the small of my back. His sweater is thick and gray and I want to lean into it, into him.

"I'm sorry I'm late," I say, trying my hardest to control my voice so it doesn't shake, revealing how nervous I really am. "That it took so long for me to get here," I say, knowing I'm fumbling my words. "I mean, I hope I'm not too late in deciding to join you."

He takes my bag. "Not possible," he says.

He speaks to the woman at the front desk, making arrangements for another room. I keep my distance, and walk around the lobby, looking at pictures of the Mansion a hundred years ago, reading the inscriptions, taking in the views from the windows. Newer condos have been built into the hillside, the marina is filled with sailboats and I wonder if I did the right thing coming here.

Richard gives me a key to my room and says, "It's just a few doors down the hall from mine." He asks if I want to change for dinner and I shake my head so he suggests we have a drink in his room before our reservation. He carries my bag; neither of us suggests putting it in my room. We get off the elevator and I follow a few steps behind. Richard opens the door to his suite, sets my bag down. I stand in the entryway with my coat still on and watch as he opens a bottle of red wine. Two crimson couches face each other in the sitting area and there's a coffee table in between. The fireplace flickers low and gives off a scent of burning pumpkin. There's a full view of the cove and the light is changing. The ocean is darkening even more. I sit on floor, lean against the cushions. Richard gives me a glass of wine and settles on the couch across from me.

"Are you sure you're comfortable?" he asks moving the pillows on the couch, situating in.

"I like sitting on the floor," I say.

He smiles. "I've always liked that about you."

He seems more at ease than he was at the house. Maybe this is who he is outside of how I've known him, outside of an often somber, serious setting—especially in the last couple years. I'm guessing this is how he is with his friends, at dinner parties with other successful forty-somethings', wine and cocktails or expensive whiskey, smoke rings weaving through conversations about politics and agents and budgets and art.

"I'm really glad you came," he says.

I nod, cross my legs. "I got your note," I say and smile.

"I should have tried harder to persuade you to come with me. I think I've just been afraid of pushing you," he says, rubbing his forehead.

"You've been amazing to me," I say, taking a sip of wine.

"We've known each other a long time," he says. "You'd do the same for me."

I nod, thinking about what he said. Would the space I was in with Sam, just surviving, allowed me to?

"You would have," he says, reading my mind, knowing I may be questioning myself.

"I haven't asked you how things are going for you," I say. "I'm sorry I've been so selfish, so wrapped up in myself."

He looks out the window. "It's to be expected," he says. "When we are in the thick of it, it survival, I think."

"Most people don't get that," I say, quietly. "Or ever realize it."

He pours himself a glass of wine.

"Are you seeing anyone?" I ask, and feel my pulse quicken— wanting to know the answer and not wanting to. I set my glass down hard, not meaning to.

"I was," he says.

"Was it serious?" I ask.

He laughs, as if I'm being ridiculous. "Now, here come the questions," he says.

I shrug. "I think I never had the courage to ask before," I say, surprised at my honesty. I think I only wanted to or was only capable of seeing him a certain way or in a certain light: calm, controlled, well-dressed, ambitious, successful, reliable, one dimensional. I think I sensed that if I allowed myself to know anymore, I would have to feel all the complications that came with it.

"Are you confused why you're here?" he asks. "Or you want to know why I asked you here?"

I shake my head, sit up straighter. "No, I'm just curious about you. What's going on," I say. "Sometimes I feel I don't know that much about you. It's not like you say a lot about yourself, at least your personal life."

He nods, as if he'll accept that for now.

I look around the room, at my bag right by the door.

After a while he says, "To answer your question, no. I wasn't in love with her."

Something about the way he says it, or how long it took to answer, I don't know if I believe him. Was she still around, or in his life, or calling, or waiting for him to come back from the island, come back from me?

"What happened?" I ask. I tuck my hair behind my ears and my hands shake.

"She didn't understand the amount of time I was spending with you. And then me coming up here." He looks at me for a long time.

"I understand," I say. Did others see things about us before we did? I know that if I'm going to have a chance at figuring this out, figuring him out, what's happening, I need to say, ask all the things I think I can't. "Were you in love my mother?" It must be the wine, or something finally lifting, a haze around me. But it's a confidence, a new kind.

He leans forward, sets his glass on the table and rests his elbows on his knees. He stares at something on the coffee table as if he needs time to carefully pick his words. He shakes his head. "I was infatuated with Isabelle for a while," he says finally. "I was younger than her, twenty-five, it was the first time I'd been out with an older woman. I thought her ambivalence was just her playing hard to get." He laughs. "It wasn't."

I look away and try to push the image of them out of my head. Images of them I've had and wondered about. I feel like the young girl again, jealous of the beautiful mother winning all the attention in the room, knowing I could never compete with her, even if she wanted me to.

"Ask me what else you want to know," he says. "Let's get this out."

"Maybe I don't want to know," I say, feeling the anxiety, wondering if there are certain things I could never accept or get over.

"Isabelle wasn't interested in me," he says. "It was a few dates at most."

"You slept with her," I say, because I can't ask. The statement is easier to get out.

He shakes his head. "I think she was involved with someone else at the time; her head wasn't in it." He takes a sip of wine and looks at me in the eyes. "I wanted to," he says and he closes his eyes and I can picture the twenty-five-year-old boy-man.

I don't know what to say and I think I would have preferred he say they had. His wanting of her, never getting her—it feels worse.

I look at him and squint. "So, have you always wondered what could have been?" I sound agitated, yet I can't help but question if I'm here because my mother isn't, or didn't want to be.

"Not at all," he says. "I think because you were so young at the time, you pictured it or saw it a bigger deal than it was."

I cough, my throat feels dry. I think about all the times that Isabelle implied they were lovers, had something deep and long-lost. Is it because she knew or sensed I felt something for him? That she knew her power and felt it over him? Over me?

"I always thought she hurt you, that you never got over her," I say. I drink my wine, finish it, reach over and fill up my glass and his.

"No way," he says. "Probably what you were sensing is something else."

My legs are asleep, tingling, but I'm afraid to move.

"I was with someone for a long time," he says. He leans back, adjusts the pillows as if he can't get comfortable. "I cheated on her," he says. "Didn't treat her right."

I nod. I recognize the look on his face, I've seen it on mine—regret, disgust, loving the wrong person in the wrong way, or loving the right person in the wrong way or staying too long.

"Then she got sick," he says. "And I stayed." He stretches out his arm, rests it on the cushions. "She got better, beat it. But it was a long hard process. She was very ill for a long time." He crosses his legs and twirls the wine in his glass. "I felt horrible that I resented her for the years it took from both of our lives."

All I can think is he never said anything, never once. He never said, 'I know how you feel, I've been through stuff,' or 'Hang on,' or 'You aren't the only one whose endured lost years.' He never gave me instructions, told me how to make it easier or the grieving shorter.

We take a sip of wine, then set the glasses down and then pick them back up. The sun has set. The fire had gone out, the room is shadowed but we didn't notice.

I wait for him to say more, but he doesn't. "I feel like when you lose everything, you eventually have a choice," I say. "You go on or you don't. Sink or swim. But if you go on, are you ever the same?"

He taps his foot under the coffee table. "I don't think you're ever the same," he says. "But that can be a good thing."

There's no longer light in the room. I can only see the outline of him across from me. Eventually he starts to talk again, as if he needs to, as if he needs to admit to me who he was at certain times in his life, that he didn't like it, that he was ashamed. I listen as he tells me about her, that they fought all the time, that she knew he didn't love her the same way she loved him, that even though they both knew it, neither left. She made crepes on Saturdays; they went away every Easter to a town called Carefree in the desert with her parents. She insisted they visit church there. And even though he wasn't religious, he found spirituality there—in a church built into the base of a boulder.

When the phone rings, I don't think he's going to answer it but eventually he gets up, turns on a lamp and picks it up.

"Our dinner reservations confirmed for a half hour from now. At Christy's," he says. "It's a hole-on-the wall above a psychic shop with a great view of the Eastsound."

He re-lights the fireplace. "We've been talking in the dark."

"You're right," I say. "We have been."

Candles glow in white votives. The smells of meat, vegetables, basil glaze and sweet potatoes waft around us. We drink more wine, a dry merlot. I feel dizzy. I look at Richard. The candlelight flickers all around, reflects off his face and his dark sweater makes his hair appear jet black. I think about how we dressed at the hotel. Even though I had my own room, I changed in his. We passed a tube of toothpaste back and forth, I watched from the bedroom as he pulled on a shirt, saw a flesh-colored tattoo in Sanskrit below his shoulder blade I'd never seen. I'd put on mascara as he put on his shoes and socks—remembering that there's something so intimate about sharing a room with someone, with him. As we walked through the lobby, out of the hotel, I fought the urge to reach for his hand. I felt beautiful as he helped me into the car, and watched me slip on my jacket.

I feel him backing off the conversation.

"Again, I really appreciate you coming up here. I know you've never been away this long."

He crosses his arms, leans in as if he's going to tell me something.

"How can I say thank you enough," I say, feeling tears fill my eyes.

"I should get you drunk more often," he says, smiling, his voice low.

"I mean it," I say. "You've been so consistent. This whole time. You don't waver."

"I care about you," he says. "And I'd like to figure out what this is between us."

"I don't want to go back to L.A.," I say. Or to films, or to houses I once lived in. I want to be honest with him, where I'm at—terrified, not able to imagine sharing a life with someone again.

"I assumed that," he says. "I think it's pretty natural to feel that right now. Scared. Unsure."

Most people in the restaurant have left. Plates and glasses are being cleared and washed.

"You're different up here," he says leaning back in his chair. "I can't see you wanting to leave this."

Is that why he hasn't left? Does he think if he leaves, he may never find this part of me again?

"You've stopped fighting everything," he says. "Fighting happiness or being content. Not being the person, you think everyone expects you to be."

"My hair's different, too," I say, running my fingers through it. My attempt to lighten the mood falling flat. Instead of laughing, he stares.

He moves my wine glass away. "Let's get out of here." He motions for the check.

"When are you going back to L.A.?" I ask him.

He walks around to my chair as if to help me up. "Why do you ask that now?" he asks.

He starts to walk away, then stops, changes his mind. He comes back. I stand up, grab my purse. He leans in, shakes his head, "It's okay to be scared. I am, too." He kisses me. I take a deep breathe in, taste his breathe, the smell of wine and his cologne and he pulls me in tighter. I wrap my arms around him, I can't get close enough.

After a while, he pulls away and he says, "I forgot my phone. I'll go ask the hostess to call for a ride back." He walks away, his hands in his pockets and I realize I'm still leaning forward slightly, waiting for something more.

It's completely black outside, and in the car, I can barely see him, but I feel him, the weight of his body heavy next mine as he kisses me in the back seat. When we walk up the hotel steps, we stumble, and look at each other. Inside, we keep our distance and walk through the lobby, past the concierge. In the elevator, he takes my hand again and I rest my head on his shoulder, loving the softness of his coat against my cheek. In front of the door, he fumbles with the key to his room. There's a brief moment that I think I'll let go, walk the other way. Then the latch clicks and Richard takes a step inside, extends his hand and pulls me gently, his deep voice whispering my name.

CHAPTER

NINETEEN

t's the first time I can remember not being able to speak, to say anything, even forgetting the vibration in my throat. I even spoke at Sam's memorial, told a story about us when we were children. About losing my footing at twelve years old and falling into dark water. How Sam pulled me out and onto a splintered dock—long before I felt safe to swim on my own.

Richard steps on the brakes hard, as if there is something in the road, but there isn't. He continues along, drives slowly, towards the ferry landing. We're on our way back to the house on San Juan. I look down at my hand, white-knuckled, gripping the leather seat under me. I can't help but notice my finger, empty, where my wedding ring used to be. The tan line is completely gone, erasing any evidence it was ever there.

I have a flash of last night, Richard's lips on mine, a hint of dinner mints still on his breath, our mouths tasting the same, red wine and sweet potatoes. His face buried in my neck, as if he couldn't get close enough to me, holding on to me, whispering my name over and over, each time sounding different, a musical rhythm luring me in more and more.

His cell phone rings again and pulls me from my thoughts. I can tell it's his assistant director, the tone muffled; Richard's voice rises, a sense of urgency that I can't remember ever hearing. I try and focus on what he's saying—problems with the writers and the script behind deadline.

You have to get back right away; I almost say aloud. But he and I know this already. I think about earlier this morning, lying in bed with him, my head on his stomach as he spoke on the phone. His body tense, quick breaths, his right knee bent as I traced the large scar there. I'd gotten up when I heard him say he could be on an evening flight. I felt his hand on my back, then he reached for my arm, urging me to lie back down, to stay. I'd gathered my clothes before he could tell me we had to leave or he had to leave. I went in the bathroom, pulled on one of the robes, sat on the tiled floor as the shower ran, beads and trails of water on glass, steam climbing the mirrors.

Richard hangs up the phone, asks how I'm feeling, if I need anything, or if I want to stop for some food. I feel cared for, looked after and it's a new feeling, one I'm not used to.

"Doing fine," I say, but I'm not. It feels like whatever we had in that room overlooking the bay is slipping away and the life of Los Angeles is seeping in as if that phone call had burst the bubble that surrounded us. It was a poke of reality. He was leaving, had to return to a place I no longer wanted to go.

"I will come back," Richard says. "As soon as I can. This should only take a few days."

We look at each other. "Nothing has changed, Eva," he says, and reaches over for my hand.

"I don't know how much longer I'll stay up here," I say, my hand clutching the leather seat tighter. It feels easier to separate now, to end it before it gets more complicated. He was always going to have to go back.

He leans towards me as if he can't hear me. There's silence as he makes a turn towards the ferry launch. The sky clear, the smell of the ocean is strong, almost offensive with hints of dead fish and rooting kelp.

"I wouldn't be going if it weren't absolutely necessary," he says after a while and he runs his hand through his hair.

I nod. I know this, or tell myself I do. But I've heard it before, people I've loved have said the same thing. Isabelle said it to me once, and years later, Sam did too. Neither came back. I get out of the car. "I'll get the tickets," I say, shutting the door and I don't turn around, even when I know he's waiting for me to look at him.

Sam was eight days older than me. No matter how old I got, or we got, he always told me I acted too young. Countless times he called me a child, or insinuated I wasn't what he expected of a woman. Over the years it became loud and clear all the ways he felt I failed him. It all chipped away at me. At first slowly, almost unnoticeably and then towards the end of our relationship it accelerated. I stopped speaking up for myself completely, started dressing different, my voice even started sounding different, almost toneless. The voice in my head started sounding like Sam's—deep, negative, deprecating to the point of pounding.

I take a seat by the window on the second floor of the ferry. It's taking Richard a long time to park the car. My view faces west and I think about if Sam were still alive, how long it would have taken him to really leave me, file divorce papers. How he'd say that it just wasn't working out. He believed I couldn't handle adult situations properly even when my birthday candles lit twenty-eight and then twenty-nine. I couldn't grocery shop adequately; didn't know how to pick the ripest, organic fruits, boil pasta like the Italians, with swirls of measured oil and floating pepper. I never seemed to wear my hair back tight enough, like he preferred, like elegant Spanish women with long necks and small concerned lines across olive foreheads. Wisps would always fall loose onto my face. I was never as small as his mother, could never bear to accompany him to lunches with his friends or ex-girlfriends, sit there, smile, as they called each other nicknames. I burned bagels, especially the thickest half, he'd always leave it untouched on a paper towel, and the crumbs smeared black. My desperation to please him never ceased.

The more he complained, the harder I tried, until I stopped recognizing myself. When I passed by a mirror, the reflection didn't look like me. My hair was straightened and flat, wearing revealing clothes, sunken-in cheekbones. His power over me created this tunnel vision, the panic of being left by him ceasing all my logic. It felt like someone was pushing me under water and holding me there, arms flailing, grabbing, fighting. Never stopping to think I could put my legs down, push off the bottom and surface, free of the drowning hold.

When Richard comes up behind me, I don't turn. His voice is soft, talking to someone on the phone, again. He sits down next to me, his cashmere coat brushing against my hand. I try and picture going back to the house on the island, how it will be. Chilled tile floors, drawn curtains, freshly made beds by a cleaning service I've never seen. Or would it be as I left it: a full coffee mug on the kitchen counter, the sliding door open, a foggy breeze, jackets and blankets jumbled on my bed. Would Grace be there? Would she wonder where I'd been?

Richard hangs up and looks at me a while before he speaks. "I'm sorry. The timing is the worst."

I nod. "It is."

"Just be patient with me," he says, crossing his legs and setting his arm behind my back. "Stay in this," he says, his voice low.

It all looks and sounds like a script I've read or done: the scene where the leading man's leaving, wearing the right thing, saying the right thing, the lighting's perfect, the backdrop making you breathless. I know the part, what I'm supposed to say back. My hair swept over my shoulder, lips stained pink, eyes hopeful, trusting.

He takes my hand.

"I don't know what's next," I say, smelling stale coffee and muffins that have just been ripped out of plastic wrappers. "It's probably better that you're going back," I say. "Give us some time to think."

"What scares you? Your mother or Grace? What they'll think?" He runs his hand over my cheek and then brushes my hair back out of my eyes. "I can talk to Isabelle. To both of them."

"Not yet," I say.

Like the leading man in the script, is he too perfect, his lines are predictable, too kind—oblivious to the magnitude of the situation. I know how I'm supposed to feel: filled up with butterflies and on the edge of love. Instead, it all makes me uneasy and I stare at him.

He nods and looks away. "Got it."

The outline of San Juan Island is ahead, a fishing boat is trolling next to us; a captain's hand goes up as a horn blows. "Kris is about ready to have the baby," I say.

"Another reason for you to be up here," he says and starts dialing on his cell phone.

A voice comes over the intercom for passengers to return to their vehicles on the lower deck. Richard says hello to someone on the phone and stands, motions that we should get going for the car. I'm suddenly panicked, as if what we had or are about to have will be over once we get off this ferry. Will the reality of setting foot back on land ground us. Will the mundaneness of real life, jobs, decisions that need to be made, locations, other people, and the past rush in, like the tide, bringing in sand and trash, muddying the clarity of the water? Or if we leave this boat, will it reveal this was just a situational enchantment one that grew amidst mystical surroundings of tall, dripping evergreens, navy blue sea water, lingering rain shadow and white humming ferry boats? Or will we come to find that this is something real that's been building long before we knew it? Was it a foundation forming, hardening beneath our feet that we weren't able to feel until we were strong enough to stand on our own? I pull gently on his coat as he starts to walk away.

He turns, holds the phone away from his ear as the person on the other end continues to talk. "Eva?" he asks.

I want to say, let's go back the other way, to the hotel.

He reaches out his hand. I take it and close my coat tighter around me. "There's a plane that leaves for SeaTac at noon," I say softly. "And flights from there to L.A. every hour."

"Got it," he says, and I'm not sure if its to me or the person on the phone.

CHAPTER
TWENTY

As I wait in the kitchen, pretending to study the mail I'm holding, I hear Richard walking upstairs, back and forth between the bed and the closet, packing. They are long drawn -out footsteps, and consistent, as if he can't put his things together fast enough. Then his suitcase wheels trail along wood floors.

He'd headed straight upstairs when we returned from Orcas Island. Most of his things were already packed, as if he'd predicted his imminent departure. Did he anticipate a call would come from L.A. or know his days here were winding down.

"I'm going to get going," he says coming into the kitchen, putting on his jacket. His hair wet and combed back. It hasn't been that way since he first came.

"Make sure the sliding doors are locked at night," he says, looking past me, out the kitchen windows.

I look down at the catalogue gripped in my hand.

"Did you hear me?" he says. "I'm going to get going," he searches for something in his pockets.

I nod. It's all I can seem to do. He's so cold. Distant. "I'll call when I arrive," he says, saying all the proper things, like always. "Do you want me to stop by the beach to see how things are at the house?" he asks.

I shake my head. "Lily's been checking on the house. Staying there some."

"I am really sorry, Eva, if happened like this," he says. "The timing. Me having to get back." He takes a step closer to me. "But I am aiming to return by mid-week. And we can have the time to talk this out."

Even though I know, I can remember so well that when people in our business are called, they go—I can't seem to make it easier for him or me, give him the reassurance we both need. Am I completely grasping, using this as an excuse to put the distance I can't ask for? "The line at the ferry backs up at this time, all the commuters. You better get going," I say, setting the mail down on the table.

He's standing so still, shoulders back, bag at his side, dark blue buttoned-down shirt, and his New Balance sneakers replaced by square-toed black leather shoes. It's the outfit he arrived in.

"Don't do this, Eva," he says. "You're pulling away and it's so hard for me to leave." He shifts his weight from side to side.

"Send me a text when you arrive," I say, unable to help it. I feel the anger rising inside me—anger at him, at the circumstances, at myself. I haven't felt genuine, out of control anger since I can remember. I seemed to skip that stage of grief. Everyone told me it was supposed to come; I keep waiting for it.

He pauses as if he's going to argue or say something to put me at ease. Instead, he puts on his dark grey cashmere scarf and adjusts his collar. "Do you want me to stay?" he asks, clearly frustrated. "Just say it. Or dammit just come with me." He crosses his arms.

"Go." I say. "It's fine."

"Okay," he says and walks towards the door.

Isn't he supposed to be the one that stays, talks, takes my hand until I feel better? That's how it has always been. His hand, so much bigger than mine, encompassing it, his voice smooth and rhythmic, calming me, reassuring me with his choice words, the wisdom always quiet and simple, lingering long after he's gone. I look at him, know that if I just reach out, touch him, surrender, everything will be instantly better. But I can't, my mind and my heart, torn, forced onto two different trajectories. And me, standing in the middle of them, at the crossroads, knowing I have to choose one to go with, to trust one path.

"Aren't you forgetting your role, Richard?" My voice low, I don't recognize it.

"What's my role, Eva? Remind me," he says, crossing his arms.

I pick up the mail again and continue to sort it, separate everything into piles according to their size and shape. "You fix things. People. Are you done trying to fix me?" I separate envelopes, catalogues and coupons, knowing exactly what I'm doing, unable to stop myself.

He squints and it seems he's going to say something mean but he stops himself. Instead, he says, "I'll call when I land." He walks to the door.

"Richard," I say, hearing the anger in my voice.

"Don't," he says, not turning around.

He opens the front door; the sky is no longer blue. I follow him outside and stand on the steps as he loads the trunk. When he's done, he looks at me, shakes his head, then opens the car and gets in. It would feel better if he yelled at me, called me names, like Sam used to. But he says nothing. I can't imagine him gone, can't imagine the house not smelling like soy marinated fish or buttered artichokes or seeing his melted ice cream in a coffee mug in the morning.

"Richard," I say.

He starts the car and rolls down the window. "You want to fight. Why are you doing this," he asks. "I don't know what else to do. I told you I could come back in a few days. That doesn't seem to be enough for you."

I walk down the steps, open the passenger door and get in the car.

"Go inside, Eva" he says, putting on his seat belt.

"Don't talk to me like I'm a child," I say, shuttering at the sound of my own voice. High-pitched and whining.

"I have to go," he says. "I feel like you want to fight, to say the worst possible things but I'm not interested. I'm not him, Eva." He looks out the driver's window.

I stare at his profile, notice the crow's feet, how they fan out perfectly from the corner of his eye, like the rays we used to draw on suns as children. "Say it, Richard," I say, shifting in my seat. I close my eyes and picture Sam, outside the car, shaking his head at me, mouthing something, but I can't make out what it would be. I can only see the disgust on his face, the disappointment.

Richard shakes his head and lets out a breath.

"Didn't you hear anything I said?" he asks. "I'm not him, Eva."

I ignore it. I can't stand to hear that—can't stand that he's right but that I can't logically process it. I can't separate them yet. "Say that it's too much, Richard," I tell him. "Say it'll never work."

"This is exactly what I was afraid of." He leans over me and for a second, I think he's going to put his arms around me. "I'll speak to you when I get back home," he says as he grabs my door handle and pushes the door open.

The air rushes in so cold, and I'm hit with a concentrated smell of decaying seaweed. I start to cry.

He hits the steering wheel hard in complete frustration and the hollow sound startles me. "Go back in the house, Eva," he says, quietly.

I can't make myself move. The car idles, straining. I hear the phone ringing inside, the message inbox full of many messages from people I was trying to forget, or put off. His disappointment in me is paralyzing me to the point I feel like dead weight in the seat.

Richard puts his head on the steering wheel and I can't bear this, to see him defeated. I'm crying harder, not understanding the fight, anger, panic, fear, why it seems to be sitting on top of me. Why I can't control what I say, why I've been telling him to go when I want the opposite. "Please come back, when your business is done," I say.

"I don't think you know what the hell you want," he says.

I wait for him to straighten up and pick up his head. But he doesn't and I can't look anymore. "You need to figure things out," he says. "And stop hiding up here. Do something."

His words stop my breath. It feels like I've been punched in the gut, but there's no mark or indent of impact to prove it ever happened. I close my eyes and hang my head because he's right. He's always been right. And it's not just up here that I've been hiding, and it's not just since Sam's death. I was hiding before, from the truth, from myself, from people's insight into my choices, my husband, the way he treated me. I dressed my unhappiness up in a beautiful house, the right clothes, and an accomplished career. All the while, what I couldn't face always lingered beneath the surface, hid around the corner, seeped into the foundation, an insidious black mold that climbed through the walls of my life and relationships. Like a disease growing silently, strengthening, my ignorance gave it time to spread and infect. And when it finally revealed itself, when it was at its most deadly and toxic, I didn't even try to fight it. I was the oblivious, feeble swimmer that saw the crest of the rogue wave too late, willingly letting it swallow me on its way to pound the shore.

He finally leans back in the seat, takes a deep breath, as if he knows there's nothing left to say.

"Maybe you're right," I say. "About everything." I get out of the car, and don't shut the door. Moments later, I hear his tires along the slick driveway as the rain that had been hovering, idling above within a smeared charcoal sky, starts to fall.

I knock hard on the door. The carved bronze cuts at my knuckles, but I keep knocking. Kris answers, her tee-shirt is riding up her belly and her skin's aglow in the dim entryway. She motions me in, pulls her long cardigan around her stomach.

"I thought the weather was changing for the better," she says.

"He's gone," I say.

"I figured," she says. "I was just lying down." She has dark circles under her eyes and she walks slower. "Come lie down with me." We walk to her bedroom, down the long hallway that's lined with black and white pictures of family members, old and young.

She lies down, as I stand near the end of her bed. She pulls a blanket over her. Her eyes lowering, hair fastened up in a topknot.

"I'm so tired," she says, putting a hand on her stomach.

"You're getting close," I say. I notice all the baby books, pink pamphlets, information, crib instructions stacked on the bedside table.

"About 6 weeks left," she says.

"Can I get you anything?" I ask. It's a relief at the idea of caring for her.

She shakes her head and pats the space next to her.

I feel squirmy, remembering all the times I stood at the edge of Isabelle's bed as she lay there, sleeping, or staring at the T.V., curtains drawn, her black hair over to one side, blanket tucked under her chin. How I would wait for her to ask me to lie with her, or hope she'd drift off, so I could slip under the comforter and curl in unnoticed. I tried to avoid at all costs her waking and saying, "You're too old for this, Eva," even though I wasn't yet six, seven, eight.

Kris turns on her side, positioning herself and winces, as if it hurts her. I climb on the bed and rest my head on a pillow. "He had to go back for business," I say, looking at the wall. "He said he'd come back. I told him not to, but then changed my mind. It was a mess. And basically he doesn't think I'm ready for what's happening."

"You're ready," she says. "Almost." She's making circles around her stomach, like she's rubbing in lotion that's not there. "You just have to get over the fear or thinking it'll end badly."

"He's not coming back," I say, turning on my side, my back to the window, to the view of rain bouncing off the water. "I pretty much fixed that. I said all the things that make people go away."

Kris curls her legs up. "At least you realize it." She reaches out and touches my hand. "Are you ready to go back to L.A.?" she asks. "To go after him?"

I picture my house in Malibu, the shower curtain that I special-ordered for Sam, the black and white hand-painted map of the world. I see traffic, billboards, a line of smog smeared above Santa Monica, the dirtiness, the stained murals in Venice.

I shake my head. "No," I answer. "I don't think so."

"A little distance might be good," she says. "Take some time to figure things out. What the next step is for your life. What you want to do about your career. It'll come."

"That's what he said," I say.

My cell phone chimes in the pocket of my sweater. A text message. My stomach churns but I don't move.

"Do you want me to check it," Kris asks.

I shake my head. I reach for it, stare at the dark screen, hope so much it's him—that if I touch the button, it will reveal his name, his reassuring words in Times New Roman font—words of regret or longing. Kris's eyes are on me and I hit the message icon and then that sinking feeling returns when it's not his number.

"It's Grace," I whisper. "She's heading back to the island soon."

"It'll be good to see her," she says.

"Richard told me I was hiding up here," I say, embarrassed, and ashamed that he's right.

"You needed to for a while," she says. "To regroup, to get some perspective. Things are changing." She pulls a blanket over her feet. "There has to be a time limit on hiding, though."

"What if he forgets me?" I ask.

She reaches out her hand, brushes the hair out of my eyes and smiles. "That's not possible."

I want to believe her, tell her that hasn't always been the case. People have forgotten me. I scoot closer and put my head on her shoulder. I feel the tears spill over my eyes, and I can't believe I'm crying again, unable to recall a time in my life that I couldn't control the tears or decide when to turn them on and off. For so long I've used them to portray someone else's, some characters heartbreak or happiness. But it's different now. I feel myself, my emotions coming through raw and uncovered.

I keep waiting for Kris to move away, or get up, but she doesn't. She takes my hand and squeezes and I look around the room, the walls, painted a warm beige, there's an ivory quilted chaise in the corner, an open book on it, as if someone got up, mid page. Soft chenille blankets cover both of us, and the scent of apricot blossom wafts from honey-colored roses in a large sea glass vase. Hers is a house I don't want to leave, like the inside of a womb, filled with a shielding, insulating, weightless warm liquid.

CHAPTER
TWENTY-ONE

My kitchen is so empty, but filled with things. Pots hang from the ceiling casting shadows and the cabinets are filled with plates, every shape of dish for pasta, curry, sushi, butter and lobster. I sit down at the table. I miss hearing Richard's footsteps coming down the stairs or his mug being set down on the black walnut wood of the kitchen table. I miss watching as he leafs through the newspaper and folds it back when he finds something interesting.

It's been a long two weeks since he left, each day dragging into the next. It's the first time I've been alone in a while. There's no one handing me something, checking what room I'm in, asking me to go for a walk, or ride to the post office for stamps. Is this loneliness? But a new kind? I was so familiar with being lonely in a relationship, with someone next to me. That's a different kind of ache than I'm feeling now. This is a specific loneliness because I'm without someone—he's missing. I'm missing him.

The phone rings again and I don't answer. I look at Richard's gray scarf still hanging on the coat tree. I haven't had the courage to move it. I haven't had the courage to call him either, neither of us has. His words, what he said before I left the car, so fresh in my mind, so uncomfortable. *Do something, Eva.* He's always been right; even though there were countless times I chose not to listen or pretended not to hear. I think about our conversation right after Sam died, it was he who predicted what was to come. He had stood next to me, leaning against the kitchen counter, at the funeral wake, his tie loosed around the collar of his black shirt. He spoke low as I cut melon and then bread and artichokes. People milled in the living room, within a hum of chatter and Jeff Buckley's voice coming so softly through the music system, singing about a satisfied mind. Richard had looked at me, "It's going to hurt like hell. And it will probably get worse for a while. You have to sit on your hands, feel it, the pain. Don't reach for anything. Not self- help books, booze or other people. It's the only way, Eva, to come out the other side."

The iPad rings from the living room, pulling me from my thoughts. My first instinct is to let it go. But the phone just rang and I have that uneasy feeling that something's wrong. The consistent ring gets louder as I get closer to the coffee table. I see Isabelle's face on the screen. Her dark hair is pulled back and she's looking down at something. I stare at the *accept* and *decline* button, know I only have seconds to make a choice. I hear Dr. Rose's voice in my head, her words from our last phone session. "Baby steps, Eva. Every time you face something you don't think you can, that's where the growth and healing surges."

I sit down on the couch, the dark velvet warms my bare legs. I adjust my sweatshirt; it's slipped down off one of my shoulders. I pick up the iPad, hit *accept* and take a deep breath.

"Why haven't you been answering," Isabelle says. She's just put lipstick on, her mouth has a fresh red tint and her face is illuminated against the darkness of the kitchen. She's sitting at her kitchen table, and even though I can't see it, a beautiful chandelier hangs above her. The draping crystal strands glittering from the reflection of the New York skyline lights outside her windows.

"Sorry," I say. "You're right." I'm surprised at my answer. I'm not making any excuses, spurting half-truths, my heart isn't racing.

"How are you?" she asks, and pick up a glass of water and take a long sip. "Haven't heard much from you apart from the texts."

She has a dramatic side part and her hair sweeps across her forehead accentuating her sculpted eyebrows, dramatic and dark. When she smiles, her cheekbones rise.

She doesn't give me a chance to respond. "We just got in from the theatre," she says. "Saw Hugh Jackman's new play."

I nod. "I've heard good reviews on that."

She takes another sip of wine and her antique chandelier earrings gently swing back and forth. "It was phenomenal," she says.

I nod again, feeling nerves heightening, wondering if she can tell by looking at my face that things have changed, that something's different. I look outside the window, the sun about to set, hovering above the distant trees. I feel that being up here, in this fresh oceanic air, three hundred and sixty degrees of natural beauty surrounding me—it's been stripping away anything fake or staged about me. My willingness to put on a face or pretend is slowly peeling away as if the sea air is corroding and breaking down the walls I've constructed or façade I've learned to hide behind. Like it does eventually to the paint and wood of the houses that sit on its shore.

"Richards's gone now?" she asks, looking straight into the camera.

"Yes," is all I can answer. How does she know? Have they talked? The thought makes my heart race.

"I assumed." She turns and looks at something in the room. I hear a male voice. She says something softly to Patrick that I can't make out. Her face softens. I can tell she's happy with him and most likely their relationship intensified when she returned from visiting me. She's let him move in—the first man she's let live with her since my father. He's good for her. From what I can tell, what she's told me, he's strong, accomplished, he stands up to her. He appreciates her independence and sophistication. In our last conversation, when I'd told her that he seems to accept her, as she is, she'd nodded, looked away and said, "That's all we can really ask for, Eva."

"Everything okay?" she asks.

"I'm doing a lot better," I say and look straight at her.

She nods. "I can see that," she says. She looks relieved.

"Have you been thinking any about your next step?" She does her best to seem nonchalant but her voice has a hint of tension that she can't mask.

She's always pushed me. Since I was small. Pushed me at times before I was ready. But what's different now is she seems to be aware of it, trying her best to ease in, without a lecture or a judgment.

"I got an email from Russ the other day," I say, carefully, looking at the mug on the coffee table, the day-old teabag floating, enlarged and puffy. "He has a script he really wants me to read."

She takes another sip of her water and I can see a small smile behind her glass. Her large almond shape eyes are still and beautiful as if she's staring at something, studying something she hasn't seen in a long time—taking in all she's missed.

"I'm thinking about telling him to send it up," I say, softly, the thought of a script arriving at the front door terrifying and exciting me all at once. I glance out at the kayakers that are just beyond my dock, slowly paddling by. They are laughing. One waits for the other to catch up to him.

"I think that's a good thing," Isabelle says, setting down her empty glass. "Just ease in as much as you can."

Her voice is soft and encouraging, the way she was those last few minutes in the airport all those months ago. I can still feel the imprint of her hand in mine, not wanting to let go. Whatever shifted then between us, I still feel it, despite the miles. It gives me strength and a confidence I haven't felt from her before. Was this the beginning of that mothering, nurturing love? The one I saw friends being the recipient of, heard about from colleagues, studied in a lot of the scripts I took? A kind of love that makes you feel like you can do things you never thought possible. A love that waits and concedes, a home you can always return to no matter how much time has passed. I'm almost afraid to hope.

"I will," I say. Is this the time to tell her about Richard? To ask for her guidance or wisdom? To ask her to tell me what the right thing to do is?

"Is there anything else?" she asks.

I scoot to the edge of the couch, feel the iPad shake a little in my hands. I can see my facial expression in the tiny box in the corner of the screen. My skin looks paler, my smile lines deeper, my forehead creased and worried.

Before I can say anything, she says, "You'll know when the right time is. For everything."

The screen gets darker and I focus on her tone. How sure it is, like there's no other option. She has always been so hard on me, hard on herself. Her calmness now, the gentleness, the encouragement, it almost makes me uncomfortable, it's almost painful. I don't know what to do with it, or how to accept it.

I nod, and I feel the tears filling my eyes.

"You're going to be okay," she says softly, looking away.

I look at my face in the tiny box again. Tears are rolling down. My eyes are wide open, my pupils whiter. There's no sound.

"I didn't always make it easy for you," she says and she sits up straighter, squares her shoulders back and her eyes darken. She purses her lips and her cheeks hollow. Her demeanor hardens slightly. I know she can't say much more and maybe she never will.

I hear Dr. Rose's voice in my head again. How she said that in life, we can't wait for apologies from those who've wounded us. We have to go on and not let the shadow of what never was hover over, paralyzing us in the darkness it carries. But she also said that if it does come one day, to accept it in whatever form or tone it arrives in. Even if the apology is wilted with limitations, and not the grandiose performance we wished for and built up in our heads—receive it.

"It's okay," I say and stop myself before I call her Isabelle. Realizing that it may not be appropriate anymore, that it hurts her, hurts us. It's a name with so much attached to it, a reminder of what we both missed out on.

"I love you," I say and look straight into the camera. She can't look back at me, but that's okay. She hears me.

She nods. "Me, too."

I let out a deep breath. I know she means it.

"I'd like to come visit when you know where you're going to be," she says.

I hear footsteps and see Patrick's hand on her shoulder and he leans down and says hi into the camera. I say hi back and smile as their faces press together.

"I'll let you know when I talk to Russ and figure it out," I say.

"Get some rest," she says. She looks away.

Her profile is beautiful, the city lights aglow behind her and she signs off and the screen goes to black.

CHAPTER
TWENTY-TWO

The script sits on the coffee table in front of me, a torn Fed Ex envelope cast aside, just where I left it last night when it arrived. The title, typed simply in courier font, is small and almost swallowed up by the whiteness of the page. "BRINGING TOMORROW," stares back at me.

Russ had told me briefly about the story and the character. He said she was an inner city teacher from a prominent family who falls in love with an ex-gang member and father of one of her students. It will shoot in New York and some in Canada. He reminded me I'd met the director, David, before at a screening party a few years ago. He's a Paul Thomas Anderson–type, in his thirties and this is his third independent film. The last one was the buzz movie at the Telluride Film Festival and bought by Plan B Entertainment, he'd said. When I'd asked him about them insuring me, or if David was concerned, he'd cut me off, afraid for us to get too far ahead of ourselves and said, "It's not like you were in Promises Rehab, Eva. Or hit someone while high. He's fine with everything. In fact I think it makes you more intriguing to him." And I could tell he didn't want to talk about it anymore, harbor on the details now, that it would come later, when it was time. The focus was getting me to put a script in my hands again and see how it felt.

I run my hand over the title and let my fingers leaf through the pages. I see her name, SARAH EVERLY, and without meaning to, I instantly wonder about her. Who is she? Where is she? Who are her parents? Grandparents? Where did she go to college? Why did she want to teach? What does she want? What has had a huge effect on her life that brought her to this point? Who is she underneath? What does she need to overcome and can she do it?

And it all comes back to me. It feels familiar, as if the wonder and this process never left—the desire to know the character, the instant connection, the anticipation of starting on the inside of her and working towards the outside. I want to dig for who she is, to discover what makes her come to life and then get out of the way.

I look out the window, at the lone sailboat anchored a few hundred yards off shore. The early morning light casts a lemon glow off the water. The surface is so still that it looks like a glass mirror, reflecting everything that hovers above it. I can't help but wonder and hope this process will be different this time around. Before, when the shooting was done, and the film wrapped, I wasn't anxious to shed the characters after having let them live with me so long. I wasn't excited to be rid of them and go back to me, my life, my house. I was never in any hurry to go back to wearing my clothes, driving my car, or having to return to my conflict, my relationships. It was much easier, much more inviting to stay and face theirs—to imitate emotion instead of really feeling it. I think of Richard, of this house, of Isabelle, Grace and Kris and know, with certainty, that I will be eager to come back to them.

I settle back into the couch and put my head phones on, set my iPod to Jeff Buckley and open the script to the first page. I let the music clear the thoughts and fears from my mind and take a deep breath and began to read:

EXT. A STREET IN JAMAICA, QUEENS- EARLY MORNING.

∽

A car pulls in the driveway. It has to be Grace. I haven't spoken to her, only had missed calls followed by texts, each one postponing her return here another day. The last one said, *Eva, I'll be there, most likely Saturday.* I assumed she was just coming back for her things, and the distance, the month she's been away, had done something to her or to us.

There's a knock at the door. I don't get up from the couch because she has a key.

"Didn't you hear me?" Grace asks, setting down her purse on the chest in the entryway. I know by looking at her the temperature's dropped outside, her cheeks are flushed and her hands are pink and clenched. Her hair is darker, longer, her bangs are shorter and her lips are chapped and peeling. A sign that the wind off the Sound has been rough on her.

"I was on the phone," I say. I want to stand, give her a hug. We haven't been apart this long since she came to Malibu. But her body language is tense and arms are crossed, so I don't.

"Richard's gone," she says, looking around and then immediately goes to the kitchen, fills a teapot and puts it on the stove. "How long have you been alone?"

"Three weeks or so," I say, trying to sound casual, her question stinging and making me angry—as if she didn't think I could handle the silent house. "Did you finish your school work?"

She nods, and comes and sits next to me. I sip my tea even though it's been cold for hours.

"My thesis is almost done, I just have one more class to take first session of summer," she says.

"And then graduation," I say, realizing what I'm about to say, then stop myself—Sam would be so proud. I feel sad for her; he won't see it. The first person to get a Master's in her family.

She winces, as if she knows what I'm thinking.

"Why'd Richard leave?" she asks and crosses her legs.

"Work," I say. "He had to get back." There is no response from her so I get up, touch her shoulder as I pass but she doesn't reach out for me.

"How long do you plan on staying up here?" she asks.

I feel like I could cry. She's so distant, like Sam used to get after I'd been away filming. It always took him days even a week to warm back up to me, to allow our routine to resume. I always knew when it was back to normal when I felt his arm rest on my waist in the middle of the night and then pull me closer. "I'm trying to figure that out." My hand shakes as I pick up the teapot. The water's still not warm so I set it back over the fire.

"You said you'd come up here for a month or two," Grace says, her back to me. "It's been way over that."

"I know you have to get back to Seattle," I say. I don't want to fight with her, to go in circles.

"I do need to get back," she says.

"I understand," I say. "You've gone way past the call of duty, stayed longer than you planned." I lean against the sink, not wanting to go back into the living room, sit down with her. "Everyone has."

"I have a final," she says. "I've really stretched the time."

"I understand," I say again.

"And Jake's back," she says, her voice lowering. "Think there's still something there between us."

Her voice drops and softens, so I walk back to the sofa and sit. I haven't heard her mention her ex in a while.

"He's been in Costa Rica for the past year and a half," she says.

I nod. "I remember." In the months before Sam's death, she would call him late at night in tears, conflicted whether to go join him or stay and start her Master's program. No matter what time it was, he would grab the phone and say, "Go back to sleep, Eva." He'd leave the room and close the door to the office behind him.

"I didn't think he'd come back," she says.

"I did," I say.

"He wants to try again," she says.

"What do you want," I ask, using my finger to stir the loose tea floating in the mug.

Her chin tilts up, and her eyes widen. "I don't' know. I'm taking my time," she says.

She reminds me of her brother, how he sounded when he wasn't quite sure.

The phone rings again, but neither of us moves to answer it. Our habit for the last few months. When it rang, we'd look at each other across the room and smile. We were creating our own little cocoon, and we didn't want anyone or any reality to infiltrate it. But it's changed now. We both know we can't stay that way, up here for much longer. Like it or not we are being pulled back into the world.

"Is Richard coming back?" Grace asks.

I shrug, sip my tea and don't want her to know I'm worried I'll never see him again or terrified he will never look at me the same.

"Do you want him to come back?" she asks, staring at me.

Something has changed in her. Her confidence, directness, like she suddenly wants to ask all the questions she's been holding onto for months. Or maybe it's her confidence in me. She senses I can take it now.

"He really cares about you, Eva," she says. Her eyes are so clear that I look away.

She slides closer to me on the couch and grabs one of the throw pillows and hugs it to her. "You can talk to me about it."

I can't remember the last time her voice was so soft, or the last time I saw that look she had as a little girl. She used to glance up at me when we walked, eyes hopeful, wide open. After a while she'd slip her hand in mine, play with the ring I always wore on my middle finger.

"I know you think I only had an alliance with my brother. That I never noticed things," she says.

How long have I wanted this conversation, how long I've dreaded it? How many dinner tables have I sat at with her, or car rides, or movies, thinking that moment was the right time.

"I knew who my brother was," she says, looking down.

"I loved him," I say.

She nods and whispers. "The most anyone ever loved him."

What was she admitting? That loving him, being close to him, was hard for her, too?

I picture his face, the last time he and I awoke together. He got up before me, put a robe on, went out on the balcony, and smoked a cigarette. His hair greasy and wild, his calf muscles tense and flexed. The terrycloth robe, the smoking—neither a part of his morning routine. I waited for him to come in, turn on the news, crawl back into bed but he never did. He left fruit out for me downstairs, ripe mangos from a broken down fruit stand off of Pico Boulevard. I remember just standing there and staring at them as if I looked long enough I could decipher what it meant, the message or symbolism. I even googled mangoes, searched for their meaning. I found their significance in Hinduism and in Pakistan and the Philippians, but nothing related to Sam and me. They were *just* the last thing he ever gave me. I came to realize it was probably his attempt to leave me something sweet and innocent like he used to when we were kids. When he didn't have any words left, he gave a feeble effort to return us to a time we could never go back to.

Grace rises, the tea pot is whistling and starting to scream. She turns off the stove and stands there and looks out the window. "It looks like more rain's coming. Will it ever end?"

"Do you blame me?" I whisper. I don't trust my voice—that it won't crack or fold under the anticipation. It's been over a year that I've wanted to ask her that, months and months of trying to pick the perfect moment—as she was pouring Fruit Loops in the middle of the night when we couldn't sleep, or when she was folding laundry, or untying the boat, steadying it so I could climb in without falling.

She doesn't turn around. "For his death?"

"Maybe you think if I loved him enough, or he loved me enough, he wouldn't have taken off that night," I say, my eyes blurring. The shame in my voice is almost unbearable. It sounds like a low groan muffled and forced.

"If you loved him enough, that car wouldn't have hit him," she says, her tone so heavy with bitterness and sarcasm that I don't recognize it.

I can't see her face, but I imagine it's twisted in anger. I want to get up and run. But I hear Richard's voice in my head. *Sit with it, Eva.*

Stay with it. It's the only way to come out the other side.

"If I loved him enough, if I was a safe place he could come to, he would've gotten on a plane instead of his bike that night. Came and stayed with me for a while, cooled off," Grace says. Her self-blame matching mine.

I don't know what to say. She hangs her head, chokes on tears. I hold back my tears, think of all the times I've cried and she hasn't. It's her turn.

I wish Demetria, their mother, were here. Her dark hair would be slicked back, large green eyes soft and sweet, a crocheted lace top hanging off one of her narrow caramel-colored shoulders. She'd run her hand down her daughter's arm, tell her Sam loved her. Remind her how when they were small, he used to press his forehead to hers every night and make her sing a Spanish lullaby before bed. They'd alternate lyric for lyric. Demetria would say the right things, pause at the right times, know how to let Grace grieve with dignity.

I stand, I'm afraid. I walk to the stove, next to her. Her hands hang at her side and I take one in mine.

"I still need you, Gracie" I say. "Even though he's not here."

She nods and turns around and whispers, "Me too."

I don't need to say anything more or frantically think of what Demetria or Sam, or anyone might say to comfort her. I don't have to say that our guilt is the same, how neither makes rational sense. We've both had enough, beaten ourselves long enough. Grief, loss and anger were being the invisible belts that lashed and cut at our insides, their silent lashings that only she and I could feel. The outside world only saw the put-together exterior that covers everything.

She puts her arms around me and I hug her close, kiss the top of her forehead—what her brother used to do to us all when there's nothing left to say.

Grace grins when she sees me, her Ugg boots shuffling along the floor with her bag slung over her shoulders.

"I have a bit of a headache," she says, eyeing my plate of eggs.

I smile. I do, too. Last night, after dinner and after the rain had stopped, we'd sat outside in our pajama bottoms and parkas in the oversized patio chairs, drinking pink margaritas and then the rest of the beer. We smoked the cigarette from an old pack we'd found stashed on a shelf in a closet as the fog rolled in. She said she hadn't felt that good in a long time.

"I called a cab," she says. "I figured you'd want to sleep in."

I start to say, let me take you, but we hear a car pull up outside.

She gives me a hug, presses the side of her face against mine. She seems so tiny in my arms, breakable and I realize this is how I can honor Sam. Grace was the person he protected most, the last of his family. Now she would be in my care and we would both be in each other's. "Please let me know when you're graduating," I say.

She nods. "You'll be fine, Eva. I know that now." She turns, opens the door, and starts towards the car, her shoulders back. For a second, I feel that old panic, as if she's taking the last of Sam with her. Then I picture him walking alongside her, slightly ahead, like he used to do. He'd turn around to look back at me —raising his hand and waving once, as if to say, I've got this, see you later, not goodbye.

CHAPTER
TWENTY-THREE

board the Sea Plane at the Friday Harbor dock and I think about something Isabelle once said to me. "You can only walk a child to a certain point, Eva. The rest of the way, she has to walk alone." I was six when she first said that. She was looking down at me, as we stood on the beach, our feet disappearing in the surf, the cold water rushing past us, spraying our legs. She let go of my hand and took a few steps back. I remembered my fists clenched, counting to thirty, shuffling a little further into the water and turning around. She was walking up the beach, white gauze skirt clinging to where the water had drenched her, our cottage appearing bigger than it actually was. I knew I had to do the rest alone.

I take a deep breath as the plane pushes off the dock, the fuel heating and filling the tiny cabin. I watch the clock in the pilot's cockpit, and then we take-off. I count the minutes as the plane bounces and sways with the strong headwinds. It feels like we're dangling, like a tin ornament above the Puget Sound.

Only a forty-minute flight to Seattle and thirty-two have already passed. I think about my agent, Russ, how his flight up from L.A. will be so different—a chauffeured car or an intern driving him to L.A.X, a first class ticket, a smooth, humming jet, an air phone he'll use to call his secretary many times. I try to look ahead and not down, and focus on the horizon of translucent blue sky.

I'm already tense thinking about meeting Russ in a few hours at the hotel. It had felt like there had been ten minutes of silence when I called him last week and told him I was ready for a meeting and to look over the contract. He said he thought it was important we meet in person. He sighed when I said I wouldn't come to L.A. and he coughed when I suggested he come to the Island. His voice rose when he said he could only tolerate the Northwest for a couple of hours this time of year and wouldn't go near small planes. But his tone eventually quieted and he said, "I'll come to Seattle, only for you, Eva. That's what fifteen years will buy you."

The plane dips and I look at the three other passengers: a couple and their small child. The mother grabs the son's hand as he fiddles with some earplugs. "We're almost there," I tell her, trying to comfort her. Her eyes have been filling with tears on and off throughout the flight. "Fear of flying," she'd said at takeoff.

"You were in that movie," the cab driver says as I get into the car waiting at the airport. I keep my bag with me in the backseat. "Marriot Waterfront, please", I say hoping he won't ask questions or get out his phone and ask for a picture. "Weren't you in that movie," he asks a few minutes later. "That one in Mexico?"

I shake my head. "No, but I get that a lot," I answer as he watches me in the rearview mirror. I roll down the window as we speed along I-5, the air damp on my skin, like standing under moist pines. The Puget Sound is getting closer and then I see Elliot Bay on my right, the islands barely visible amongst layers of fog.

When the driver pulls into the Marriot and the attendant approaches the cab door, I want to put my hand up, tell him, wait, give me a minute, I'm not ready. But he's already opened the door, and brisk air hits my face. I head into the lobby quickly with my head down, the bill of the New York Yankees baseball hat pulled low over my face. Tuscan Chandeliers are lit inside the hotel entrance despite it being mid-morning and the Italian fused glass evokes deep shades of autumn light throughout.

I check in under Lucille Jones. The receptionist hands me a key to a Waterfront Suite and asks if I'd like a reservation for dinner. I shake my head and then walk towards the elevator. The pianist in the corner looks up and smiles as I pass.

From the living room of the suite, I watch as the last ferry of the day approaches the harbor, filled with commuters, SUVs, tourists and tired fishermen. It's a massive white ship colored with dark green trim. Its wake produces small swells that fan out across the bay. The Olympic Range doesn't seem too far off into the horizon. The sky is clearing to a light gray after the recent a cell of rain. Room service sets up a white table on the black and cream rug near the balcony. There are plates filled with brie, baguettes, fruit, sashimi, prosciutto, melon, Champagne and wine. I wanted to surprise Russ. Countless times he picked up a check at dinner, took care of me, especially after a bad review in the trades.

Candles flicker throughout the sitting room, and I don't miss the house on the Island like I thought I would. This change feels like a relief, I don't have to try to avoid the kitchen where Richard and I last fought, or look at the front door that he closed gently instead of slammed on his way out. I don't have to wonder why the phone isn't ringing or why it is—no one knows I'm here, in Seattle, except Russ and Grace.

Russ knocks on the door a few minutes before six. The fog delayed his take-off for over an hour. I sit up straight in the love seat, running my hands over the soft zebra printed fabric, remembering to put my shoulders back, hands in my lap, tilt up my chin. Isabelle always says that's a sign of confidence, even if you don't feel it.

"You look good," Russ says, letting himself in with his key. He goes straight to the table, sets down his bag and pours a glass of Pinot. He doesn't come over to greet me, hug me, kiss me on both cheeks like most in our business. I've gotten used to it. Since I've known him, I don't remember ever touching him. He always said, "I'm not a hugger. It's easier that way."

181

He takes off his black jacket, and adjusts his black sweater tucked into black slacks. His stomach protrudes over his belt and his hair is cropped short and shiny gray. "You look really good, actually," he says handing me a glass of wine, and then sits directly across me on the sofa chair. He leans back, takes a deep breath, like it's an end to a long day.

I touch the ends of my hair. "My style's a little different, I guess." I glance down at my leather pants, stilettos and white sweater. My hair longer and darker than it's ever been. I felt like dressing up for the city. It's been a long time since I've worn anything but jeans, or work-out tights or running shoes. All fabrics thermal, flannel and heavy cotton. Head to toe in Columbia, Patagonia and North Face.

"I don't think that's all that's different about you, my dear," he says, smiling and crossing his leg.

I want to ask him to explain, I'm intrigue but instead I smile.

"No one in L.A. has heard a word from you," he says, and he looks away, seeming hurt.

"You've heard from me," I say. "We've been in touch the whole time."

"Through e-mail," he answers quickly.

"I'm sorry," I say.

He nods, as if he accepts it and will drop the guilt trip. He takes a sip of wine.

"I drove by your house the other day, when I was out in Malibu for a meeting," he says. He takes another sip. "It looks closed up."

I nod. This time of year it always looked closed up, no matter if someone was there or not. The mustard color covers are over the outdoor furniture, kayaks put away in the shed along the side of the house, boards stashed under the pilings, resting on hard-packed freezing cold sand.

"I half expected to see a for sale sign," he says.

"I've been thinking about it," I say. I haven't told anyone that. I wasn't quite sure if I was ready to sell it. Caught between not wanting the memories and everything it stood for, and not knowing if I could let it go.

"I e-mailed my Realtor last week, putting some feelers out. Asking about prices, comps, how fast he thought it would sell in this market, or if he thinks I should wait," I say, twirling the dark red wine in my glass.

"There's no hurry," he says. "But the market's been turning around out there."

"I'm sorry for not staying in better touch," I say, blurting it out. I'd put him with the rest of them: agents, casting directors, people who eat at the Ivy on Saturdays and lease Range Rovers. People who post, photo-shopped Instagram shots of their seemingly perfect days and life. Looking at him now I notice his eyes are glassy, his hair has gotten grayer and I feel guilty. I should have known to separate him from everyone. He's known me since I was eighteen, fought with Isabelle about what commercials I'd do in the beginning of my career, told me to have confidence and wait for better parts, defended me, put his jacket over me in the back of the car on the way to the hospital all those months ago.

"I figured you'd resurface," he says and sets down his glass on the coffee table that divides us. He opens his bag, and pulls out his computer and a stack of papers.

"What's the damage like," I ask, crossing my legs, ready for him to say that people think I'm crazy or locked up somewhere.

He turns on the computer, shrugs as if I'm asking him how the menu was at the new restaurant on Beverly Glenn. "It's been months, Eva. Nobody thinks about it. No one's asked me anything in a while. You know how it is. Another story. It's a different time now than when you were coming up. Yes, with the media the way it is now, stories surface faster, but they die on the vine with the next big scandal."

I feel myself start to get warm under my cashmere sweater and I get up and walk to the sliding door, focus on the lights on the fishing boat coming into the harbor. I think of the premiere and all the medication in my body that night and the dizzy lights. Maybe people would be able to look at me without seeing that figure I once was. Or would I always be that picture, a pale gaunt face, eyes vacant, frozen open? The picture from the premiere that's front and center when you Google my name.

"I have the contract," he says, speaking quietly. "I had Arnie look it over, like you asked. Drove it there myself." He sets it on the coffee table.

I nod. I trust Arnie. He's been my lawyer for ten years and always looked out for me.

"He said everything looks good. They're some decent perks in there despite the tight budget. They have you at the Trump SoHo and a rental on a lake when production moves to Montreal."

I nod, again, nervous, unsure but excited. It was only two weeks ago that I reached out and said I was interested, only a week ago that Russ, David and the producer and I had a Zoom meeting, discussing the character, script, logistics at length. And when I sent the email to David saying, yes, I can't wait to play Sarah, I had to force myself to push send. I had the adolescent butterflies that start in the stomach and spread down your limbs and flutter into your fingertips. I still couldn't believe they wanted me—it was the same feeling I had over a decade ago. The same terror, anticipation and question in myself, if I could do it. Only there isn't the innocence, naiveté and hope of what's to come that insulates a young girl. I had the knowledge and wisdom to know where it could end up and all that is at stake.

The snow on the peaks of Mt. Rainier shines and glows under the darkening sky. During that Skype meeting, I kept wondering in the back of my mind how much Russ really had to sell me, what he had to say to smooth things over, pacify, convince people that my time away in the outdoors has glistened my complexion, hyper-toned my body. That everything I'd been through had given me a deeper understanding of characterization. I realize it doesn't matter now. I'm in and the rest is up to me.

I walk back to my chair. "If it's possible, I'd like to look it over. I'll sign it and send it back."

"Are you going to change your mind," he asks, punching the keys on his laptop. "Don't do that to me."

I shake my head. "Have a little faith," I say with a smile. "I'll send it with a courier service. Same day."

"I came all this way," he says, carefully navigating the trackpad on his laptop.

"You know you wanted to see me," I say, picking up my wine glass and smiling.

"You're right," he says, smiling back, not looking up from the screen.

I listen to the traffic on the streets below and can't believe I'm here. Two months ago, I thought I would never leave the Island, the house, the life—there with its coffee shop, one long line every morning, everybody's drink ready before they asked, seafood lunches, dinners and vegetable from multi-colored lush gardens by the sea.

"You okay with everything else?" he asks, closing his laptop.

I nod and wonder if I should tell him about Richard, Grace, and Isabelle and everything that has happened—that I'm starting to sleep through the night. But instead, I say, "I'm good. Getting there."

"We'll go as slow as we can," he says, putting his computer away. He stands, puts on his coat slowly, as if he expects me to change my mind. "Filming won't start for a few months. I'll meet you there, just to make sure the transition is smooth."

"Can I take you to dinner now?" I ask, careful not to say, can we celebrate. Not yet. Too much could change.

"I'm on the last direct flight out of here," he says. "It took me five hours to get here."

"I appreciate it," I say.

I walk him to the door and he puts his arm awkwardly around my shoulders. I look at him, but he's staring straight ahead. I think for a moment, wonder, what if I went with him. Hopped on a plane, rang Richard's doorbell, or drove to the Malibu house, opened the doors, so the air could blow through, bringing life back to it again.

"Really good to see you," he says, dropping his arm. "Sure you're okay, kid?" He opens the door, keeps it propped with his foot.

I pull him in for a hug, and rest my chin on his shoulder, and he doesn't pull away or tense like I always thought he would. For a second I can smell the life of Los Angeles smoke, smog, and heavy cologne always used to cover something. I squeeze him, he squeezes back. As I close the door, he's already half way down the hall and on his cell phone. I know very clearly that I have no desire to go where he's going.

෴

I smell the Seattle Pike Street Market before I see it. African coffee beans, sourdough bread pulled from an oven, rose tea, and chalky incense. I round the corner, cross the street, the sun is just coming out and it's almost noon. I make my way through the goods section on the top level, seeing turquoise, tie-dye, Peruvian blankets and rows of chunky silver and hanging wind chimes that occasionally brush against each other. I weave through the people carrying canvas grocery bags filled with an array of flowers, organic fruit and fish just pulled from the Sound. A bearded man picks at his guitar and sings an acoustic version of "Can't You See," with his eyes closed.

My hands run over fabrics in a Moroccan store, while a woman hammers silver. I buy a few tie-dyed onesies for Kris's baby. She's a week over due and will be here any day now. I pass rows of sunflowers, tulips, orchids, lilies, roses so inviting, I want to buy bouquet after bouquet.

Grace sits by the café window and her black hair is down, straight and frames her face perfectly. Her hands are folded, as if she's nervous. She gets up to kiss my cheeks, both sides—Sam did that, too, never forgetting their mother's European traditions.

"I can't believe you came," she says, handing me a menu.

Locals sit at the bar in the back of the restaurant, and just beyond our window, there are lofts and warehouses stacked above the harbor.

"Either can I," I answer, smiling. I catch a scent of men's cologne that reminds me of Richard and I wonder if he's working or if he's on his way to the office or soundstage, or stuck in traffic. Is the sun reflecting sharply off the Wilshire office buildings, the glare in his eyes? Does he ever think of the nights we spent hours on the phone when I was secluded in Malibu? Both of us would be half-asleep, he, still in his suit, his cell phone propped against his cheek, exhausted.

Does he know that I knew when he'd start to drift off, the lapses between answers longer and then eventually, one-word replies? His voice would become soft, like a young child. Did he know that I'd hang up content? I'd tucked him in from miles away.

"Eva." Grace is looking at me, intensely. "Do you know what you want to order? I'm starved."

I can't stop staring at her, her voice so confident. She's older, mature. Just in the weeks since she left, she's different, as if the house on the island had aged her. As if being around me, and grief and Sam's memory forced something out of her that she wasn't sure she was ready for.

"Coffee and an avocado cheese omelet," I say to the waitress and I notice a couple staring at me from a corner table. I put my head down and focus on the passing ferries, their wakes leaving zigzags on the water.

"Are you going to tell me what you're doing in town?" Grace takes a sip of her orange juice. "I almost fell off my chair when you told me you were coming." She smiles behind her glass.

"I had a meeting with Russ."

"You're going back," she says in disbelief, her eyes widening.

I think about the house in Malibu, sitting on that beach, the fog around it in the winter making it seem like an Eastern European coastline—it was a symbol of a grander life that I don't have or want anymore.

I shake my head. "I'm not going back to L.A."

"I can't picture you there anymore," Grace says, staring down the couple in the corner. Her brother used to do the same thing.

"I found a script," I say, putting my hands around the warm mug. "We'll film in New York and Canada, but not for another few months or so."

She looks down into her drink, then out the window, then back at me. "It'll be coming on two years," she says and stops and I know she can't or doesn't know how to say it still—since Sam died. "It's time you get back."

I nod. I agree.

"Where are you going to live?"

"I haven't gotten that far," I say.

"You like it where you are," she says. "It's become your sanctuary. Whether you meant it to or not."

"You think?" I ask her. Maybe it was.

I stay quiet while the waitress sets down the food, steam rising off the fresh eggs.

"There are a few great places for sale near it. I like that side of the island," she says. "And Kris is there." She blows on her eggs and takes a bite.

She's telling me to move, to start fresh. Turn in the keys to the island house I'm in now. The one we arrived to months ago, when we were all different people.

"And you'd be close, too," I say. "Just a short plane or ferry ride."

She nods and shifts in her seat.

"I never thanked you enough," I say. "You pulled me through it. It wasn't easy for you. You were in your own kind of pain." She's cutting her food into small bites, avoiding my eyes. I'm reminded again in the little ways she's still like Sam. No matter how close we got at times, how far we'd come, they were both more comfortable with the unspoken. Overt affection, words saturated in meaning made them squirm in their chairs.

"Gracie," I say. "I love you."

She nods and her bangs fall in her eyes. "I know." Her eyes tear up. She pushes her plate away. "How long can you stay in town?" she asks. "Stay at least another night, two."

I nod. "Do you want to stay with me at the hotel?" I ask her. I think about those nights as kids that we laid in Isabelle's bed when she was out for the evening. We watched movies on VHS tapes, old quilts Isabelle saved from her childhood covering us, the fireplace blazing, the T.V. loud long after we'd fallen asleep, wrappers and water rings on the nightstand. Time with Grace was the closest I ever knew to what having a sister was like. Those nights made it more bearable, dulled the ache I had of wanting a sibling or traditional family that had dinners at six around a table, did the dishes together, each with a specific job. Those families would put a bag of popcorn in the microwave and race to the couch before the favorite sitcom started and Mom and Dad would give a five-minute warning before it was time to change into pajamas and brush teeth. Neither Grace or I had a family where everyone went to bed at the same time and had a dog that slept on the woven entryway rug, protecting them.

"When's the last time you talked to Richard?" she asks as she gets her wallet out to pay.

I look out the window. In the distance, I can see the dark clouds moving in and the sky is a chalky gray. "It's been a while," I say. "We had a fight."

She nods. "You get that the ball's in your court, right?" she asks, pulling out a credit card. "It's up to you what happens next with you guys."

I shrug. I already know.

"It's all in your head," she says, "You think I'll be upset, that Isabelle will."

I bite my lip.

"I'd be happy for you," she says. "If you two were together."

I fold my napkin and then fold it again.

"How come everyone's allowed to be happy but you?" Grace says, sliding her chair in closer to the table.

Her question is a good one. It's one I haven't had the answer to, but one I'm starting to figure out. "I don't think he'll forgive me," I say. "I just wasn't ready for all of that to happen. Instead of having the courage to say that, I took the easy way out. Didn't handle it well, at all."

Grace nods and brushes her hair out of her face. "And now?" she asks.

Her cell phone rings, her face changes when she recognizes the number. *Give me a second,* it says. She turns away and talks in a voice I've never heard, an octave lower. By the way she's breathing, quick and shallow, her heart is racing. She's excited and scared.

I remember that—what it feels like to be tied up in knots with anticipation, the sound of the voice you want to hear quickening your pulse. Every week that's gone by since Richard left, I've spent time daydreaming, imagining what he's doing, at all hours, but especially in the mornings because that's his favorite time of day. Even though I've let fear stop me from picking up the phone, the visuals of him have comforted me: his early morning routine, running the Santa Monica Stairs at six a.m., then coffee at Peet's, light on the milk, then home where he makes eggs sunny side up, running over toast, the *Wall Street Journal* laid out in front of him, and Bob Dylan coming through the surround sound.

She hangs up the phone. "Let me stop by and get some stuff at my place, and I'll meet you at your hotel," she says and opens her purse.

I smile and watch her as she looks and digs for her lipstick. I realize that it was pointless to spend those years wishing for a certain kind of family. I had one in front of me—unconventional, wayward, with a structure so shaky at times it left us wondering if and when everything would fall. But I know now that you take, accept what and who you're given. The rest is up to you. You create the village, the family. You invite and fill it with people and things that will allow it to sustain and grow. It's the love, understanding, mercy and acceptance that's the epicenter, the fire pit that everyone gathers around to keep warm. And forgiveness is the firekeeper.

CHAPTER

TWENTY-FOUR

I open the curtains, the sun giving the water a cherry glow. The morning kayakers aren't out yet, but the fishermen are already on their way home. The house is even quieter than I imagined it would be.

Everybody is gone, packed bags, gotten in cars, on planes, waved goodbye to me in two different houses, in two different states, went back to Metropolitan cities, no signs of islands and ferries and fields of alpacas. Their lives resumed, moving forward, in research labs, or on soundstages, or in hip restaurants and galas on the Upper East Side. Grace, Richard, Isabelle, I feel their absence, separately, in different ways. They each left for a reason, at the right time. Maybe sensing that if they stayed longer, they could cause more harm than good and I would remain comfortable, on idle, content on letting them walk a few steps ahead of me, shielding me from what and wasn't about to come.

Grace has been back in Seattle for a while, the phone doesn't ring as often; the dishwasher is never full—only the top row stacked with mugs and glasses. Her empty room is shadowed at the end of the hall. I head downstairs thinking about Kris's husbands call at five this morning. He'd whispered, "Our little girl was born two hours ago. Thank God it was a quick labor." I remember thinking that if I wasn't so tired, I would have cried.

My cell phone vibrates on the counter as I wait for the coffee to brew. I think of the gold disc necklace I got Kris, how I need to have it engraved with the baby's name as soon as I know it. I catch my breath as I grab the phone and see it's a text from Richard. Part of me doesn't want to read it, having not spoken to him in weeks, the distance widening. He'd e-mailed once, I didn't answer. My hand shakes as I lift my cup and glance at the message:

In Vancouver scouting. Stopping over on my way back. Need to talk. Probably tonight, around 7. Hope you'll be there.

I set the phone down and step back immediately, can't imagine seeing him, facing him. I look at the cell again and know if I leave it there it will be so much easier. I could pretend I never received it and maybe not responding will naturally discourage him from coming.

I start towards the staircase, picture Richard in Vancouver, bundled in a North Face jacket, his rectangle-framed glasses sliding down his nose, saying something about the vegetation or the local wine or asking about weather patterns and variations this time of year. I turn around, grab the phone and keep it clutched in my hand as I take the stairs two at a time.

I keep my head down as I walk into Inter Island Medical Center. The last conversation I had with Kris about Richard was yesterday morning. When I'd said I hadn't talked to him, she let out a small sigh and said, "Just put it all in a toy boat, Eva. The pain, the past, what you can't change." Then she muffled the receiver, the phone line filled with static. "Walk down to the beach," she continued. "Wait until the tide is going out and push it out to sea." Before I could respond, or attempt to ask her to elaborate, she stopped me and said, "I think I just had a contraction. I'll call you back."

Even before I get to her room, I smell the baby. Oils and lavender lotion, sterile gloves and starched cotton blankets. I see Kris first, her eyes wide, hair damp and slicked straight back, two perfect natural strokes of color on her cheeks. The room is pink: pink flowers, pink sheets, pink circles on curtains, pink scrubs on the nurses.

Ryan gives Kris the baby and hugs me for a long time and says, "Thanks for coming, Eva. She's been waiting for you." He pulls up a chair next to the bed. I sit, wordless, overwhelmed, taking in all of it. Kris tilts the baby up, her face barely peeking through the white blanket she's swaddled in.

She looks up at Ryan and he nods. "Meet Sola Marie," she says, her eyes happy, glinting.

I feel them both staring at me. All I can think to say is, "That was *her* name," I whisper.

Kris nods, smiles, a thick strand of her wet hair falls forward. "You said it means peace."

"In Pashto," I say quickly. "You remembered." I look away, worried that I'm breathing too loud, that in a second, I might start gasping for breath, my heart pounding, rising in my chest. That name makes me recall things I haven't wanted to—things that I'm afraid will take me back, set be back about how my body felt when I decided on that name for my little girl to be. I was standing in the shower, aching breasts, my stomach just starting to show, strands of silver water running down, falling around it. I'd put my hand on the small bulge and my mind went instantly to a film I'd done two years before. I'd played a war reporter and we shot a few scenes in a mock Afghan refugee camp. I remember the actress who played the woman I was interviewing. She had large dark eyes and a gauzy red jeweled head scarf draped over her silky black hair. When she was speaking Pashto, I kept hearing 'sola' over and over, the sound like a metrical pattern in a poem. Her voice was smooth and the lyrical language accentuated that word until it stood apart in my head. After the scene wrapped, I'd asked her what it meant. She took my hand and smiled and said, "Peace."

"Oh my God," Kris says, looking at my face. The pink flush that was on her cheeks has disappeared. "Eva, I didn't mean to—"

"But that's my name," I say, my voice is a whisper and I don't even know who I'm talking to. That's the name I chose when I imagined what my daughter would look like—a French mouth, Irish hair, Spanish skin. A mix of my mother, father, Demetria, Sam, me.

"I might still want it someday," I say. "Use it." But that wasn't true. I could never bear that.

Kris starts to cry.

"When did I tell you about that name?" I ask. I suddenly can't remember anything. I can't remember even talking about her, allowing myself to think about her.

"That night we were cooking dinner right after Christmas, you guys were drinking wine," Kris says, wiping her tears away. She glances down, adjusts the blanket around the baby's face, and strokes her cheek, her hand shakes a little. "You told us when you were first pregnant you knew you'd have a girl and that her name would be Sola."

I nod. Kris looks over a Ryan. His hands are buried deep in his pockets and his face is flushed. He's at a loss of what to do and I feel bad for him.

I hurt. It's not fair. None of it was. I'm angry. Maybe I'll always be. Maybe that's okay.

Kris looks at Ryan and says, "Give us a second."

He nods awkwardly at both of us. "I'll go get some coffee," he says and then leaves the room. "

"Please, Eva," Kris says. "Don't do this. Don't be mad. I can't stand it."

I put my head in my hands. It's the first time in a long time that I can remember wanting to scream—loud and piercing until people get scared. I want to scream at Kris, at someone, at myself.

"Please, Eva," Kris says again, her tears falling slow and consistent. "I did it to honor her, you. I'll change it. It's not on the birth certificate yet."

I finally look at her just as the baby attempts to open her eyes, like she senses something important. They are the same shape as her mother's and the color of the deep end of a dark-bottom pool. I wait for the baby to cry, but she doesn't. They both appear to be waiting for me to say something.

"I should have asked," Kris continues, shutting her eyes. "I should have asked."

"You should have," I say, shifting in my seat, uncrossing my arms. I instantly feel guilty for my harshness. I look at her, lying so still in her bed, in pain, sore, her eyes tired with a hint of dark circles underneath. An I.V. needle taped over her hand. Whatever I'm feeling—the anger, envy, sorrow, I need to place it where it belongs. On myself.

Kris leans forward, stretches her arms out with the baby to give her to me. "Will you think of a name, then?" she says, starting to cry again.

My first thought, no, I won't pick one. I have no name to give her. I gave up on names, I'd picked one before, it had come to me so easily but it didn't work out. And until now, I'd forgotten about the process, the thought too painful. Like something you shove in the back of the closet that you know you'll never use again but just can't bear to give away.

I make myself reach out and take the baby. She feels so tiny, weightless, delicate. Under the thin blanket, I can feel her legs tucked up, her arms folded over her heart. The smell, intoxicating and I lean in closer. Like left over pieces of pancake sunk in the freshest maple syrup. The warmth like hot stones.

Out of the corner of my eye, I see Kris relax into the mattress, the tension leaves her hands and she rests her cheek on the pillow. She keeps her gaze on us even though she's fighting to keep her eyes open. The baby shifts in my arms, curls up more and I feel the anger, the sadness, the ache start to disappear. I hear Dr. Rose's voice, again, it seeming to surface right when I'm about to walk through something that hurts. *As hard as it is, Eva, you have to believe that it wasn't the right time, wasn't supposed to be. A miscarriage, it's nature's way of protecting all of us in the long run. You have to let go of the blame, my dear.*

As I look at the baby starting to drift off to sleep again, I suddenly have such a clear picture in my mind, of watching her grow up. All of us on South Beach, looking out at the Strait of Juan De Fuca, the Olympic Mountains, appearing to be resting atop a thick line of cotton clouds. I can see a woven Mexican blanket spread out, shovels, buckets and food covering it. We're bundled up, but our jeans are rolled to our calves, feet freezing, soaked and sticky with sand, picking up tumbled sea glass and things washed in from the Sound.

"Okay," I say firmly, gesturing to the baby. "Her name is Sola." And as soon as the words leave me, I feel a weight lifting or the dormant heaviness that's been in the pit of my stomach shattering like impacted glass and falling away. It's as if the releasing of the name to her was the final sidekick that burst open the hidden, sealed door. The rush of fresh breeze and air and sun roars in. The suffocating, stale stench is overwhelmed and beaten. Ventilation and light restores a balance, allowing me and the memory to walk out.

Kris closes her eyes, and nods, fighting back more tears. She's so tired, and it looks like she's finally giving into the sleep she's been fighting. Until everyone and everything was okay. "Will you stay?" she asks.

"Of course," I say. "I don't think I could leave if I tried."

We both smile and don't have to say anything more. We understand what we've just been through: an accidental naming ceremony. A death and a birth, encompassed a resurrecting, bestowing, surrendering and handing off of a name once so weighted in loss. That name now holds sudden life and a hope of new beginnings. One that means peace, so how could I not let it go, give it to someone, a family that has brought me exactly that.

Soon, Kris drifts off to sleep, her arms draped elegantly and protectively over her stomach. I watch her and the baby both, their breathing echoing each other's in exhaustion and calm.

As I drive home from the clinic, I still feel lighter, like I lost weight or took off a backpack I'd been carrying up a steep side of a mountain, heavy with supplies that I'd need just in case. The heat swirls in the car and touches my cheeks. There's a powdery scent that circulates and my sweater smells like Sola. The up and down of emotion I hadn't been prepared to face leaves me tired and exhausted. My arms ache slightly from holding her in one position for so long. The instant relief I felt when I agreed to her new name is beginning to wear off. There's a nervousness in the back of my mind. I know it's going to hurt, especially for a while. Every time I say the name will

I wonder what it would have been like if she were mine? Would I constantly be calculating how old she would be? If her hair would have grown into towhead ringlets like Sam and I both had as babies? Or maybe it will get easier, each time, healing a little more, a reminder, a lesson that loss doesn't have to injure us forever.

I look at the clock, how long was I there? It's seven-thirty, it'll be dark soon. The time flew, especially those two hours Kris and Sola slept. I sat there, listening to them, to monitors beeping, the hum of distant T.V.s in other rooms, and rubber soles hurrying along hospital carpet. Not wanting to be anywhere else.

I brake and my cell phone slides along the passenger seat. A reminder that it's there, that I'd left it in the car all day. I turn into Roche Harbor and have the sinking feeling because I never texted Richard back or called. I completely forgot. The hospital room was like a heated bubble with no trace of time. What would I have said? *Don't come. Do. I'm not ready to talk. I am. I'm not embarrassed about how I reacted. I am embarrassed. Ashamed.* I see a light on the second floor of the house even before I turn in the driveway. A blue sedan is parked in front. Not Richard's usual choice.

"I left you three messages," Richard says, as I open the front door. I don't set my purse down.

The morning after Sam died, I pulled his clothes from his closet, put them in plastic bags and then dumped them out again, onto the bed. Then I went to sleep for two days, waking once in a while when I'd rolled over on something—the lump of a wadded sport coat, the scratch of a sweater or my face in a tee shirt, his smell almost choking me.

I think of that now as Richard leans against the counter of my kitchen, his arms crossed, and he doesn't meet my gaze. Do I have the strength to possibly endure that again? To let myself love someone, especially to the extent that I imagine I could love him, and then have it all fall apart? It feels like I'm on an edge of a cliff looking down at the most translucent, bluest, ocean, and Richard is treading water below having already jumped. His hair is slicked back, motioning for me to join him. His eyes are gentle, reassuring. My brain shouts do it, jump, anticipating what it could feel like once I'm there with him. I will feel warm, crisp water enveloping me, gently breaking my fall, then his hands, strong and secure, will surround my waist, guiding me to the surface. The current rocks us as he holds me. But my heart screams louder; that first step-off is too terrifying, the risk too great. I could slip on the push-off, tumbling forward, or hit a protruding part of the cliff that I can't yet see or misjudge the distance down. My speed could pick up in the great free fall, no ability to slow it, no position safe or protective enough as I'd hit the water. At that speed, the surface would be like unforgiving concrete, shattering everything I have left from the inside out.

"Stay awhile," Richard says, gesturing to my grip on my purse. He's so relaxed, the sleeves of his soft black button-down shirt rolled up, and he unfolds his arms, puts his hands in the pockets of his jeans. He looks at me like he never left.

I focus on the pear tree just beyond the window, the cream blossoms turning chalky as it grows darker outside. "I'm not ready to talk, get into what happened," I say. "I'm tired. I know you came all this way. I'm sorry."

He makes a noise, it seems like a laugh, but there's no smile. "I finished up my trip earlier than I thought. You won't return my calls. I felt bad about the way things were left."

I take a step towards him, a natural reflex, and then stop. There's a birthmark right above his collar, in the soft part of his neck, just below the ear. It smells like white chocolate. "I can't ever go back there, to L.A., to that house," I say. I want to put my head down, admit that for so long I thought I failed in L.A., used up all the fresh starts, married the wrong man there, lost my family there, went crazy there. For a while I worried that every scruffy man who wandered the beach or a Venice alley was Sam.

"I get that," he says. "At the same time, that doesn't give you an excuse to push me away, to say the things you did."

I know that now is when I should apologize, maybe break down and admit how embarrassed I am, how much I miss him. I should tell him I understand why he left when he did, that it was the best thing for me and for him. I'm scared. But if I relent now, give into this, to him, what would it be like commuting back and forth to L.A.? Being away from the Island? Stuck at Hollywood parties, or being afraid to go outside, run into certain people, answer questions? Would I have to do an interview, get on twitter, Instagram, put up a website? Would I be back where I started, unhappy because of the relationship I'm in, restless because of all I had to give up to be there.

He puts his hands deeper in his pockets. "I just came here to see how you are. That you're okay." He jangles the keys, as if that's a warning he's going to leave. "I can see we're still in different places."

"What does that mean?" I ask, still frozen in place, my jacket on, I feel the sweat building on my lower back.

"You're not ready," he says and looks away as if he doesn't want to believe it. "You're too afraid. And there's no way for me to win against that. I'm willing to see where it goes, give it the space and time it needs. I don't need the immediate answers. It doesn't have to be defined. It's not black and white. Nothing is."

I undo two buttons on my coat. "And you think I don't get that?"

He shakes his head. "That's not what I'm saying," he says.

I set down my purse, let it drop next to my feet. I'm trying so hard to remember who I'm talking to. That it's not Sam or the faceless man that's condescending, hurtful, distant.

He straightens his posture. "It's just not constructive. This dance we're doing." He shakes his head. "Just shoot it straight, Eva."

"I am," I say, my voice weakening. I shake my head. I can't even pretend or convince either of us. My acting skills falling wayside, I can't even access them. I can't even imitate someone who's confident, sure of what they're saying.

"My objective in coming here was to discuss, not fight. To get to a real place. And you're obviously still angry, shut down, weeks later."

"Richard, I can't." I feel my arms go limp at my sides. The time alone, the visit in the hospital with Kris and the baby, things that made me feel stronger, independent, like I was coming out of something—they're dissipating. Richard's return brought back my fears, what I can't control. I feel weak, helpless.

He takes a few steps forward. "I believe you really think you need to find the perfect house, buy furniture, visit the cemetery x-number of times, beat yourself up hard enough, go without . . . " he says. "Before you let yourself be happy again," he says.

"Sam's wasn't buried in a cemetery." It's all I can think to say. I look at him, tears filling my eyes. This hurts so badly.

"It's simple," he says. "You're not ready to let go of him, or admit you chose wrong, that it was over long before he died, or that you aren't too blame." he says. "You'd rather punish yourself. Punish me."

"You're wrong," I say. I have started to face all those things. There's been progress. But for some reason now, I can't let him see that. My throat feels as if I'm drinking something thick and hot. "But you're saying I will be happy again, if I let myself be with you or go back to L.A., my old life."

He shakes his head. "Not at all," he says. "I'm saying as long as you stay afraid, you're going to stay trapped. No matter who you're with. Or what you decide to do."

I whisper, "Fear is normal. Part of the process."

"For a time," he says. "But then you have to let it go. Just close your eyes and jump." He jangles the keys in his pocket again.

I hear a buzzing in the room, or maybe in my ears. How could he know what I was thinking? My toes on the edge of that cliff looking out and then down at the ocean. Completely unable to step off even though I know he's not physically able to tread water, wait forever.

I look out the window, stare at the next island, wonder how far away it is, if the tide's strong, if I could swim it, and get away from here. "I think you're done here, or we're done here," I say, tripping on the words, wondering why my voice sounds like a whisper. I mean it to be loud, a shout, cutting, invasive protecting myself, my pride, my right to be unsure, afraid—not ready.

He shakes his head, "You're right, we're done here," he pushes in the chair where he must have been seated earlier, when he was waiting for me.

And all I can think is how I've hurt him. My words, my actions, my lack of actions. I picture his face after the morning we awoke together on Orcas Island—when I'd just opened my eyes, yanked my fingers from his skin as if to protect myself from burn.

He walks past me, pauses at the door. I imagine it's to give us time to change our minds, say something we know we should, preserve over ten years of friendship or prevent something that's irreversible. Neither of us speak. He slams the door. He's disappointed in me, which is worse than him being angry. I look down, still standing in the same place, the exact spot I stopped when I came in and saw him in my kitchen; looking so good, hair shaggier, his muscular thighs outlined against the slim fit of his pants, glasses on, patient, quiet, strong, forgiving. All the things I saw, have always seen—all the things he's trying to convince me I deserve.

CHAPTER
TWENTY-FIVE

From: Richard <rich.film@gmail.com>
Sent: Thursday, October 20. 2:41 AM
To: mbu.house123@gmail.com
Subject: Hey

Eva,

It has been weeks. No word from you.

And I can't sleep tonight because you infuriate me. I don't think I have ever been so mad at someone.

Even though I consciously know what you were doing—pushing me away, throwing all kinds of hurt around so I would go. I walked right into it. And then I had to rip the chord from the wall.

I know you need time and space. We both do. I know you need to learn how to trust yourself again, or maybe for the first time. To learn to trust me, in this new form—our relationship outside a realm we never entertained, beyond the friendship we always knew, or could count on.

You make me feel older at times—overly-responsible—like the guy that needs to triple check that the burner was turned off before he can walk out the door, or who needs to unpack his suitcase the moment he walks in from a Bahamian vacation. And make sure all the dirty clothes are in color coordinated piles in the washroom. You make me feel like the eighteen-year-old, young man, again. Hopeful, about to start his life, not understanding yet everything that could really go wrong. You also make me feel like the rug could yank out from under me at any moment, and the flooring would be to slick for me to catch myself. But still, I could quit everything tomorrow and hole up with you on that island. Wall off from reality, until whatever this is between us, heals us both.

That is not the path that either of us would be happy taking. Or that we should take.

What I think you still do not realize is how strong you are. The young woman I met so many years ago, when you opened the front door, was fearless. Held gazes, didn't back down or look away from anyone, forged a path to success, despite every-thing, a lack thereof—of so much you needed.

You are going to make it out the other side of all this. Whether we figure out a way through this or not, I love you. I'll be up that way in a few months. Reach out if you want to sit down and talk.

-Richard

CHAPTER
TWENTY-SIX

"I decided to put it up for sale," I say over my shoulder. Kris walks behind me, Sola asleep in a baby carrier against her chest. "My house in Malibu," I continue, as if she didn't know. I catch myself realizing I said *my* house. Not our house—Sam and mine's. She doesn't answer so I turn around, wait for her to catch up. I can't help but let out a breath, as I see the white lighthouse, behind us. It's tall, attached to a keeper's house, a red shingled roof, chalky white paint and teal trimmed windows. It's perched atop a cluster of black rocks that disappear into the ocean. The Kilm Pointe trail we're on hugs the coastline and winds along the tree covered bluffs.

She smiles, her cheeks flushed. It's so damp, the occasional spray off the ocean rests on our faces.

"I think you absolutely made the right decision," she says, brushing away the strands that have loosened from her ponytail.

"I told my realtor to sell it," I say. I picture the house's glossy dark wood floors with strips of sunlight coming through the drawn curtains, its balcony railings crusty with sea-water from a long winter. I can't imagine ever going back there, I'm afraid if I walked through the door again, I'd erase everything that's happened here, since. When the realtor told me how much I could get for it, that I'd break even or possibly get a little more, I let out a breath and was quiet for what seemed like minutes. I could hear the background noise of a restaurant or shopping mall he was at, muffled voices and distant laughter. It was the last tangible thing I had left that linked me to that life, to Sam. It was the last place we lived together. Like us, from the outside it looked sturdy, statuesque, an exterior that showcased glamour, the glass ceiling of success. Upon first glance, everything was in its right place. But like our relationship, especially towards the end, the interior was scarce, bare in places, not lived in. He never wanted it; he never thought it was home. He sat on the floor a lot instead of the couches, he had unpacked boxes shoved in the back of his custom walk-in closet. "Eva?" my realtor asked. "You still there?" I'd taken a deep breath, thought about the cottage atop the Holly-wood Hills that we lived in before we were married—hotel rooms that were much simpler, where we had periods of happiness. Those places and memories were what I could hold onto when I needed it. It's like his choice, his wish to be cremated instead of buried. He knew the people that loved him wouldn't need one place to go to remember him, feel his presence. He knew we would find him in smells, split aloe leafs and ocean air, or in his favorite places, a vacant beach, an offshore break at sunset. Not in the clothes he left behind, halls he walked down or the bed he slept in. "Sell it," I'd said.

Kris and I sit down on a bench and I run my hand over the inscription on the stone—someone's name. The waves crash against the rocks and it won't be too long before the whale watching crowds start arriving. It's finally spring.

"It's starting to stay light later," Kris says as she adjusts Sola's knit beanie. "I love it."

I can't believe it's been a month since she was born, and only two months until I'm to report to New York for rehearsals.

"I think I'm ready to buy a place up here," I say. "I heard the Holman Cottage just came up for sale."

Kris laughs. "That's hardly a cottage. Two stories, Calamander wood floors, a large boat house."

"I don't want to go back," I say.

"I know," she says. "You don't have to."

"Richard has been doing some shooting in Montreal. He's going to stop by on his way back to L.A.," I say, shifting, getting cold, the wind picking up. "Next week or the week after."

"You heard from him?" She asks, surprised.

I touch the side of the baby's cheek. "I got an email from him. It took me awhile, but I responded. Said that I'd like to see him. Then, I didn't hear back for a while. But a few days ago, I get a message that said he'd like to come to the house. So, we can talk in person."

"What did the email say?"

I take a deep breath. "Everything I wanted to hear. And needed to hear."

She looks over at me, holds my gaze and smiles. Like she already knew it would all unfold this way. "You don't have to do everything at once, you know," Kris says, pulling the blanket tighter around the baby. "Go easy on yourself."

"I was avoiding him," I say. "I needed some time, to get some perspective before I could face him again." I make a circle in the dirt with my shoe. "I owe him an apology. In person."

"I'm just saying to take it one thing at a time," Kris says. "Your house, going back to work, Richard. It's a lot."

"It's what's left for me to face," I say.

She takes my hand and squeezes, then lets go when Sola makes a sounds and shifts in her baby carrier.

I think about what she says. About turning corners, about what it feels like when you start to feel your life moving forward, pieces slowly moving together with a quiet force, towards a whole piece. I look out at the ocean, where the other islands seem to extend all the way to the horizon. "At the end, Sam wasn't the same person I fell in love with, maybe even the last few years," I say and then lower my head. "I get that now." She takes my hand again. "That person I knew when we were twenty-three, when we were kids, was gone. He'd left long before his accident."

"He was really hurtful towards you at times," she says. "It sounds like you were both unhappy."

I nod, start to cry, keep my head down. "We lived like that. For a long time."

She stands and then pulls me up with her. "It's okay now. It's over."

Sola wakes up, starts too cry, too.

"I'll call our realtor," she says. "We can start looking at places tomorrow."

Her grip on my hand is strong. My bare hand in her fuzzy glove. The feeling reminds me of getting out of the cold ocean into an oversized towel, still heated from sitting on the hot sand. Shielding, comforting and protection until you're warm enough to let it go.

"Kris," I say, the tears sticking on my cheeks.

She sways side to side, in a natural bounce as Sola starts to quiet. "Yes," she says softly as if she already knows what I'm going to say.

"Thank you." My tears start falling again. "You never even asked about everything that happened in L.A. Or about my life before. You gave me this amazing, unexpected gift. A grace that I don't think anyone has ever given me."

"People tell you things when and if they are ready," she says.

"But still," I say. "You're different. Very special."

Her eyes fill with tears. "I loved you since I met you." She smiles. "You have this thing, Eva. You make it impossible not to." She takes a step towards me and puts her arm around me and I let me head fall on her shoulder and take Sola's hand. Her little fingers clasp around my finger.

I'm not sure if the long exhale is hers or mine.

I set the table with the placemats I've never used. White glasses with blue rims and I place star gazers and white roses in a vase in the center. Tea lights surround the dark wood bowls. It's been a long time since I set a table or dressed up, heels instead of flip-flops and a dress—all of a sudden it feels like a sign of normalcy of routine—of stability.

Richard had said he'd arrive sometime between now and eight. They were flying private and they would take off as soon as the last shots were done. He'd sounded different on the phone, distant, professional and far away as if the connection was bad.

Car tires cut across gravel and then there are two swift knocks on the door. I sit and then stand, not sure what to do. I forgot to light a few of the candles in the other room. He lets himself in. He doesn't have a bag, just an overcoat and black glasses that I remember he needs to wear at night, when he drives.

"The door was open," he says.

I hold myself back, from rushing to him, hugging, feeling the scruff against my cheek, and breathe in the smells of the outside and where he's been.

"Sorry I'm late," he says. "We had trouble getting some of the shots and then we had to wait to take off."

I lean against the table, reach for the lighter.

His voice is low, strained. He looks tired, hasn't slept. "Joe flew with me. He got a room at the place by the ferry. He's fine with flying out tonight or first thing in the morning."

"You both are welcome to stay here," I say. I force myself to light the rest of the candles, try and think of something else to say. "Was the flight okay?"

"Yes," he says.

"I waited to eat," I say. "Are you hungry?"

He nods and I take the rotisserie chicken from the warming oven, take the rice from the pot and I hear him remove his jacket, listen to his footsteps, strong and hollow in the entry hall and then in the living room. He turns on music and I let out a breath—it's okay. My hands shake as I attempt to rinse the salad in the kitchen sink. His footsteps circle the downstairs in a rhythm, he knows where he is, it's familiar, it's his place.

He comes up behind me, stops, and I see our reflections in the window above the sink. I can't see his eyes. I don't turn around; I don't know what to say. I listen to the song, try to grab onto the words. He steps closer, takes off his glasses, sets them on the counter, puts his hands around my waist, and runs his other hand over my stomach. I let go of the lettuce and he turns off the running water in the sink. I feel his nose and lips behind my ear and I let my head fall back against his chest.

When I turn around, his eyes are almost closed and he breathes deeply. I lean in, hug him. He tenses, he kisses me, and his fingers press in the small of my back. When I let out a sound, he lifts up my dress and picks me up, places me onto the counter. My head hits the cold cabinet, I don't say a word—I let him strip everything from me.

The morning sunlight comes in bright into the bedroom, through the balcony doors. He's not next to me and I'm afraid to go down-stairs, see an empty kitchen, dishes done, no coat slung over a chair. As I grab a robe, step into slippers I'm listening hard for a sound, a coffee maker, a door opening. But there's nothing.

Over and over again I remember telling him, don't leave, and stay. As if I knew he needed to hear that after hearing *go* for so long. Throughout the night I kept waking and reaching out in the haziness of sleep and cold sheets to feel the other side of the bed—unable to relax until I touched his arm or lay my hand on his stomach and felt it rise and fall. Just before falling asleep for the last time, I looked at the bamboo shades, knowing I should get up, lower them. I never did.

I walk down the stairs slowly; breakfast is on the table and the patio door is open. Richard's sitting on the deck in one of the chairs, leaning back, and legs crossed. The end- of- winter air sneaks in, breezy and cold, along with the smell of kelp, burning wood and salt.

"Morning," he says, his head turning slightly as I come up behind him.

"Hi," I say, feeling shy.

He hands me a cup of coffee that's still hot. I look out at Deer Island, the multi-story houses, and Japanese gardens. "I put an offer on a place about a mile from here," I say.

He smiles as he sips his coffee.

"And I'm going back to work," I say, putting the coffee to my mouth but not drinking. I just barraged him with information. Everything I meant to tell him last night, but never got the chance.

He nods. "I ran in to David the other day. I told him you were the best choice for that role."

He knew already. "I wasn't sure what you'd say about me going back," I responded.

"You're ready," he says, his eyes following birds skimming the water in a perfect V.

"I'm sorry about the way I acted. What I've put you through," I say.

He nods. "I said some things I didn't mean. You just know how to push me."

I sit down on the ottoman facing him and look out. "I fell in love with you," I say. "I don't even know when. Years ago maybe."

He uncrosses his legs. Leans forward, put his hands on my knees. He's quiet, he knows I'm not done talking.

"I don't want to go back, though. To that life. I want to do it on my own terms. Live here, travel to locations, but always return," I say. "At least for a while. Until I get my bearings." A sea plane lands way off shore and the sound is loud, and distracting.

He scoots in more, takes the mug from me, sets it down, and pulls me onto his lap. I put my face in his neck and rest my cheek against the collar of his fleece jacket. "We'll take it as it comes," he says as he tightens his arms around me.

What he's saying, the way he says it, he's no longer the Richard I knew, back in Hollywood, before everything happened. He's not the guy always in a suit jacket who I'd see at occasional lunches, passing by one another at the studios, mutual acquaintances in common.

"Do you love me," I say, a whisper, into his jacket.

He nods and lets out a sigh. "Don't you know how much I love you?" He clears his throat.

"Tell me," I whisper.

"I love you, baby."

I bury my face deeper into his neck, the soft spot just below his ear.

"I'm scared as hell," he says, his voice cracking.

"Me too," I say.

He doesn't reply for a while and then says, "It'll get easier."

The minutes go by, curled up in his lap, and then longer and I find myself telling him things I didn't think I could, that I don't want to lose him, be without him. I don't ever want to lose the friendship—that's what brought me to where I am. I never want to lose the hours we spent sitting on that deck in Malibu, chairs aligned, looking out at the horizon, seeing the Santa Anas blowing burnt brown leaves in late fall, his hand almost touching mine and the early, pale auburn sunsets.

— CHAPTER —
TWENTY-SEVEN

From: Isabelle Douglas <isa.douglas1@gmail.com>
Sent: Thursday, October 20 2:41 AM
To: mbu.house123@gmail.com
Subject: Hello

Dear Eva,

I couldn't really talk freely during our last call because I had company. We have been playing phone tag and since I have always been better in written word, I thought I would send this. I wanted to say that I think you made the right decision to take this film. I think it's in your blood, being an actress—creating. I have thought that ever since you were a little girl. But I also think there might be other career paths, or personal paths or something else that arises from this step forward. It will come to you.

It has been a long few months since I left you in the airport in Los Angeles. I realized there are many more things I should have said that day or before or since. I think I was not who you needed during that time I stayed with you at your house after the premiere event. I feel badly. For a lot of things. I had you so young, and I was ricocheting off bad situations, bad relationships—absorbed in everything I wanted or angry about things I wished I had done… but despite me… you became this incredible woman.

I meant what I said on the phone. You are going to be okay. You *are* okay, always were.

When you get settled, I would like to come and visit and stay for an extended period, if it is okay with you.

Love,
Mom

CHAPTER
TWENTY-EIGHT

Isabelle told me once that if I lay out in the sun long enough all wounds will heal. I remember believing it, lying on my back at the beach during an Indian Summer as a child, my feet buried in the sand, trying to stand the heat as long as I could. Then, sunburned, rushing into the house, looking in the mirror, disappointed when the scrapes, bruises and fresh scars were always still there.

I feel her presence now, and think about what she said and how I was too young to grasp or decipher figurative language. She didn't mean that the sun would heal me. She was telling me if you wait long enough, can withstand discomfort, things will eventually heal on their own.

I look around the bedroom, my suitcases full and I can't close them. I ended up with more than I came with. I arrived here, on the island, with only a few clothes. The beds, coffee, curtains, and the things that felt like mine for a while—I'm to leave it all.

"I talked to Russ," Richard says, coming into the room. "You're all set. You just need to show up by next Wednesday."

I nod, smile, almost shyly. It doesn't seem real, what's about to happen. The last month I've been working so hard on the script, studying, running lines with Richard, his smile spreading wide after a scene, kissing me, his encouraging words making me feel like I could face what's to come. I will be waking before sunrise, reporting to a set, fighting to keep my eyes open after the end of the first week, the exhaustion, both emotional and physical settling in.

"You're coming the week after I get there, right?" I hear the anxiety in my voice. Even though I've known him so long, what's between us, what's been developing and deepening every day still feels new. The adrenaline rush and trailing insecurity that comes with a new relationship very present; still not wanting to be more than three feet from someone at all times. Dizzy from their smell and touch.

He sits on the edge of the bed, nods. "Yes, Eva." He says smiling. "I'll be there."

He zips up one of the suitcases. His facial hair is thicker since he arrived, his eyes rested. Our last few weeks spent walking through the farmer's markets, picking out meals, or on a porch, the BBQ filled with salmon and corn, then often untouched on our plates because we're lost in conversation. He made me fish with him some mornings, bundled up in parkas, hats, our hands always freezing. His catch was always bigger than mine. When we walked, he took my hand, and my chin fit just behind his shoulder. When he caught me staring at him, he'd wink or lean in for a kiss.

"You sure I shouldn't go back to L.A. before I go," I say. "At least until I need to be on set. Tie up loose ends on the house. Things like that?"

He shakes his head. "No. You got Russ and me handling all that," he says. "You got this, kid," he says. "No need to be nervous.

"I got this," I say, repeating his words.

He places the suitcase on the floor. "It's a good thing. Getting back out there."

I try to close up another suitcase.

"It'll only get easier from here," he says.

I nod. I believe him.

"I want to drop these suitcases at Kris's before you take me to the ferry," he says. "So you won't be tempted to come with me." He winks.

I laugh. I'm staying with her until I go. Escrow closes on my new house on the island at the end of next month.

"I already can't wait to get back here at the end of the summer," he says, as if reading my mind. He grabs two suitcases, heads for the door. "Gives us something to look forward to." I picture him in the new house, setting up his tools in the shed, building things, shelves, fences, a new door. Taking the kayaks out at sunset, our boats gliding across the glassy water, patches of citrine light coming through the break in the clouds, the air crisp, a mix of cut grass, stale sea water and squashed serviceberries.

"I'll be right down," I say, not quite ready to go. He kisses me and when he starts carrying things out, I look around the room. Sheets stripped, drawers open, the T.V. off. I close the curtains, catching a last look at the dock rocking after a boat passes, the sky, the setting sun, gold stripes across the pine treetops.

He lets go of my hand when the people in line start to move towards the ferry boat, but I want to hold on, tell him I don't think I can do this, on my own. He reaches in his pocket, puts a small velvet pouch in my hand. I look up at him and he nods for me to open it. I reach in, and there's a cool sensation of a chain. I pull it out and the light catches on a small cross covered with canary diamonds.

"For protection," he says and I know all that he's telling me that I better not even think about giving up even when he's not always going to be with me. Our careers and interests and lives will keep us apart for periods of time. And that's okay. We're two individuals who don't need each other to make it. But together, we can be stronger.

I hug him because I can't say anything, my throat hurts too much.

"I love you," he says. He kisses me and lingers. "I'm proud of you."

There's a moment where I feel myself starting to take a step forward, wishing I could board the ferry with him, go back to Malibu, drive the long stretch of Pacific Coast Highway, my hand loose on the wheel, turning it with the curves of the road, everything familiar and the same as before.

I kiss him back and our fingers intertwine as he backs away, and then turns. Disappears into the crowd. The morning sunlight reflects a balmy turquoise sheen on the water, the necklace clutched in my hand, my thumb tracing its outline. The ferry pulls away from the dock and people are frantically waving to those left on shore and I understand now. I put the cross on, feel the clasp hitch and the weight fall against my chest. I let out a deep breath. It was never about forgiving Sam or Isabelle or anyone else. It was about forgiving myself for the mistakes I've made, for having chosen wrong so many times. And then learning to accept all that has happened—accept the sadness, damage, the good things that are left inside of me—everything unseen to the outside world.

I walk on Main Street, and catch my silhouette gliding along the windows of the darkened shops, and know that down the road, I will remind myself of this day and the clarity that blew in with the pasty offshore breeze off the Sound. I will hold onto it in the times when it will get hard again, as well as to the voices of those I love, telling me to relax into the unknown.

—ACKNOWLEDGMENTS—

I want to say a special thank you to my Mom and Dad—who recognized I was a writer long before I did . . . then told me over and over to never give up until my stories saw the light. Thank you Mom, for believing in me so profoundly, and giving me the courage time and time again to keep going, when it was so much easier to stop. Your loving grace and consistent belief guided me through this artistic journey.

Thank you, Dad. Even when I got deep into a fulfilling career and furthering my education—for always saying at pivotal moments, "What about your book?"

And in that, I also heard, don't forget to stay true to who you are, that part of yourself. I am forever grateful for the powerful gift of belief you both gave me.

Les, you nurtured and championed me and this story from "go." You were tough, you were fair, you were loving just when I needed it. Of the SO many things you taught me . . . the one that lingers so profoundly is when you said, "When looking into a fire, the eyes start to really burn after awhile . . . when everyone else looks away to alleviate the discomfort . . . a writer keeps looking, because past the burn is where the good stuff lies."

Same goes for life, Les. I miss you.

Thank you, Robyn. You were the writing mentor/life raft, genuine ray of love, that came a long when I needed you most. My editor, my friend. The way you root for me, and my voice—just kept me going, page after page.

It was supposed to be.

Thank you to Robin and Liz. I know you were the ones who were meant to take me/my story the rest of the way. I'm grateful our paths crossed, and then became such a safe space.

And to our Tine. I love you so. May that very strong, curious, loving spirit always guide you to where you are meant to go.

I can't wait.

KJ's writing explores the depths and complexities of the human experience and the shared events that unexpectedly connect us. Her stories give us the opportunity to relate to ourselves and to each other, prompting us to look at life in new and authentic ways.

—— COMING SOON ——

Accepting a job teaching at an inner-city Charter School hundreds of miles away, Jane Madsen drives south towards a dream she promised her late brother she'd fulfill. She's torn, leaving a career at a thriving family agricultural business in central California, a close-knit family emerging from grief, and a broken engagement to a man she's loved since the seventh grade. At the suggestion of her father, she moves into her grandma's closed-up vacation beach cottage that hasn't been inhabited since her brother's tragic death. Immersing in a new profession and a new city, she is invigorated by the start of a purpose-filled life.

Jane quickly connects with her students and their classroom, interwoven with learning and compassion, soon becomes four walls of refuge for them all. A place that feels safeguarded to the pressing complexities of the world outside their window of broken blinds. She builds relationships with colleagues committed to the power of education and begins a quiet romance with an up and coming urban artist who volunteers his time at the school. But when an outspoken teacher is abruptly fired, cracks emerge which rapidly widen in the integrity of the school and its director. Along with a few trusted teachers, Jane uncovers past and current illegal practices of a man taking advantage of a community in which he was raised, and the parents who entrusted their children to him. Jane finds herself at the epicenter of a looming educational scandal that threatens to unravel the lives of the students, community, teachers and mission that unites them.

Book reviews help other readers discover my books.
I would appreciate it if you would consider leaving a
review on Amazon, Goodreads or your favorite review site.